EAST CHELTENHAM FREE LIBRARY
400 MYRTLE AVENUE
CHELTENHAM, PA 19012-2038

EAST CHELTENHAM FREE LIBRARY
400 Myrtle Avenue
Cheltenham, PA 19012-2038

Honor
to the
Hills

Also by Eileen Charbonneau from Tor Books

THE WOODS FAMILY SAGA
In the Time of the Wolves
The Ghosts of Stony Clove

Honor
to the
Hills

Eileen
Charbonneau

A Tom Doherty Associates Book
New York

This is a work of fiction. All the characters and events portrayed in this novel are either fictitious or are used fictitiously.

HONOR TO THE HILLS

Copyright © 1996 by Eileen Charbonneau

All rights reserved, including the right to reproduce this book, or portions thereof, in any form.

This book is printed on acid-free paper.

A Tor Book
Published by Tom Doherty Associates, Inc.
175 Fifth Avenue
New York, N.Y. 10010

Tor® is a registered trademark of Tom Doherty Associates, Inc.

Library of Congress Cataloging-in-Publication Data

Charbonneau, Eileen.
   Honor to the hills / Eileen Charbonneau. — 1st ed.
     p.   cm.
   ISBN 0-312-86094-3
   1. Mountain life—New York (State)—Catskill Mountains—
Fiction. 2. Family—New York (State)—Catskill Mountains—
Fiction. 3. Catskill Mountains (N.Y.)—Fiction. I. Title.
PS3553.H318H6   1996
813'.54—dc20   95-30027
                                            CIP

First Edition: January 1996

Printed in the United States of America

0 9 8 7 6 5 4 3 2 1

EAST CHELTENHAM FREE LIBRARY
400 MYRTLE AVENUE
CHELTENH⋯ ⋯ ⋯⋯8-2038

For my sisters and brothers: Michael,
Vincent, Marie, Peter, Kate, David,
Joseph, Tess, and Patricia, who are as
beautiful to me as our Catskills in
summer.

> We are together, no matter where we are
> We are blood and heart and spirit
> We are what makes the universe,
> Past, present, and future.
> We are light
> We are strong
> We are family
> We are brother and sister
> Mother and father
> We are children
> We thank our God
> We are love
>
> —Theresa Charbonneau Pelham

Soon a Celt will be as rare on the banks
of the Liffey as a red man on the banks
of the Hudson.

—The *London Times* during An Gorta Mór,
the Great Famine in Ireland

Acknowledgments

Many thanks to my editors, Natalia Aponte and Jonathan Schmidt, and publisher Kathleen Doherty, who convinced me to visit those hills I love again.

To Diane Michele Crawford and Dolores Oiler, Margie Rhoadhouse, Jim Green, Patricia A. Rogers, Susan Shackelford, Laurie Eakes, Gerald Kenny, Majorie Gemmill, Shelia Chapelle, Lisa and Alex deBritan, Barbara Ward Lazarsky, Janet Bixby, Jean Gold, Florence Kay, Laurie Maxwell, and Robin O'Brien, thanks for helping me to do my best to create the atmosphere in which wisdom might reveal itself.

Thanks to Jeremiah Ingalls for writing the words to the lovely Sacred Harp hymn "Honor to the Hills."

I appreciate the research assistance of the dedicated folks at the Hunter and Windham libraries, Hope Farm Press, Scott Meyer at Merritt Books, Mountain Top Historical Society, Carolyn Bennett at the Zadock Pratt Museum, Marc McCutcheon, Irish Visions, USA, Radharc Films, and the Irish American Heritage Museum in East Durham, New York.

Finally, thanks to Father Paul Healy, who, throughout our cherished quarter-century friendship, taught me the meaning of the word *blarney*, and to Father Don Doyle and predecessors, for saying the yearly mass at St. Joseph's Chapel that's kept alive the shrouded story of thirteen voiceless women.

Contents

1

HUGH DELANEY

The Catskills have nestled and protected my family for generations. In the clouds over our high valley, I see another set of mountains. Sky mountains, always changing. Sometimes they are near. They mist the ground and swirl about my skirts when I help bring in a harvest before a rain. At sunset they gather around the western horizon, shrouding it in a rose-tinted glow. Other times the clouds are distant, powerful, with their own thunderbolts and lightning. We watch them in awe.

My father, Justice Joshua Woods, says the ancient Greek people observed clouds like ours and created a world of gods and heroes. My grandfather, Daddy Asher, tells different stories. His are of Skyland. Of a woman who fell through a hole in the clouds with seeds in her pocket that started the world. My grandfather's people formed the first human paths through our mountains. But none lived here. To the Mohicans, the Catskills were sacred, a place for dreams and vision quests, not everyday dwelling. It was Daddy Asher's white ancestor, a Frenchman named DuBois, who brought his Indian wife here, where they became "the people of the woods." We carry that name still, Woods. I am Lily.

I was lost in the wondrous clouds that day at the dawning of my sixteenth summer in the year 1851. Another day, I might have noticed the stranger sooner, realized his sprightly tune was no bird's song. But I was so happy to be home again after my failed attempt to achieve higher learning. In my lap was the latest letter from my half sister,

Jane. Though I'd lasted a scant three months at Mrs. Beech's myself, Jane wished me to join her as teacher at her school for free ladies and misses of color. She'd founded the school with the legacy her Scottish father had left her. She'd planted it among Mama's downriver Griffin relatives, much to their dismay.

I loved my sister as my life. She was as brave as our mountain cats with their cubs threatened. How else could she write her treatises against slavery and on behalf of hospital and asylum reform? She even spoke publicly at the women's rights convention three years ago in Seneca Falls. How was I to explain the terror that her request inspired in me? Already today I'd escaped the big-boned boys who were making my present life as a tutor a misery. I didn't want to persevere amid adversity as Jane insisted. I wanted to leave all meanness aside and lose myself in the glorious clouds.

"Your master will string you up by that fetching braid if he catches you storytelling the sky. Would you desire that now?"

I looked down at the battered green cap, dark curls escaping it. A current of fear rode through me. No. He was not one of those spiteful boys, this stranger. "Master?" I echoed him. One thing my family can't abide is masters of any stripe. "You must be lost, sir."

"'Sir,' is it? For the likes of me?" He pulled a small box out of his pack. "These new spectacles I'm delivering for the trader are yours, then, are they?"

I jumped down from the wall. The boy was near to a man, tall and lean, too lean for his frame. And handsome, with even teeth and eyes the shining green of the leafy maples around us. Both the cadence of his speech and his pale complexion named him Irish. I felt both dim-witted and plain beside him.

"Who'd the tradesman say the spectacles were for?" I managed to ask.

"Oh, a grand lady, says he. Which was the image of yourself as you sat on that high wall with the leisure time for grand contemplation of weighty thoughts, you understand? But now, close up . . ."

"Close up?" I prompted.

"Well, no grand lady's got unmended stockings, I'm thinking. I'll look further to deliver the spectacles of this Ginny Rockwell, then."

I yanked at the striped cotton muslin of my gown, mortified. How had he seen the rip at my knee? Had my skirts flown up when I jumped off the stone wall? "Is there nothing but questions in you?" I asked, peeved now.

He cocked his head. "And who would like to know?"

That response made me smile, despite my piqued state. He laughed himself, causing distraction enough for me to snatch the small package from his hand. I kilted my skirts and ran up the hill toward Gran's place with it.

"Stop, thief!" he called out. "That's me calling card!"

I thought I'd lost him as I sprinted up the path toward the cabin nestled in the pines above our horse ring. I soon heard a language kin to my mother's Scottish lullabies. But his angry bursts were no lullabies.

I looked over the edge of the path. The stranger was climbing the red cliff face. He wasn't as fast as I would have expected, given the great length of his legs. I heard his coughing, then his stumble and slide. His coughing became splinted, pained. He wiped his mouth on a handkerchief. When he saw me, he shoved the cloth in his pocket.

"What are you stopping for?" he asked hoarsely, his chest heaving with effort. "Go on, deliver! Get you your favor from the lady of the house!"

I scrambled down until I landed beside him. "Are you sick?" I asked.

"No! Don't you be telling a body here that! I can work harder than any two men they have around this place!"

I'd provoked him enough to give me a straight-out answer, anyway. "Men? Hired men, you mean?" I asked.

"Hired men surely! Are you daft from staring at those clouds so long?"

Questions again. And rudeness. I prayed for some of my mother's quiet tolerance, my father's forbearance. "They don't hire out here."

"Who takes care of the place? Who cleans the great hall, and grooms the horses?"

"We help each other with all."

"You do?"

"Yes. Four generations we are here and about the Sutherland place."

"We? You're a Sutherland?"

"No. That's the one name none of us carry. The Sutherlands lived here before us."

"What are you called?"

"Lily. Lily Woods."

"Woods?"

"And your name," I asked, folding my arms, "if you can manage not to question your way out of it?"

"Hugh." He removed his battered cap. Pink splotches suffused his pale cheeks. "Miss."

"We're heading to my grandparents' cabin, up yonder, see? And we passed the—what did you call it? Great hall? It's where I live, with my mother, father, sister Jane when she's home resting from saving the world. Aunts and uncles and cousins live roundabout, and in town. We only hire out at planting and harvest. It's then my grandfather's soldier friends help."

"Soldiers?" His quick mind had picked up a link, I could see it. "From the second time you Yankees beat back the British? That war?"

"That's the one. Why?"

His eyes shone with hope, but he still answered my question with another one. "He's alive then, is Asher Woods?"

"Daddy Asher? He'd better be! Else we'd be visiting a ghost now."

"That's where we're going?"

"Yes."

"And if you please, Miss Woods, who is Ginny Rockwell?"

"That'd be my gran. Two of her names. She's Woods as well, like me, but her own daddy's name stuck so, even her husband calls her by it. Daddy Asher's her husband, and my grandfather. It's them you seek?"

"Maybe not, now. If there's no use for me." The hand that drifted protectively over the strap of his back satchel trembled. I heard the rattle in his breathing.

"You can give Gran her new spectacles from the tradesman, if it means all that much to you. I was only just teasing." I offered the box.

He snatched it away, as if I'd change my mind. "I . . . I beg pardon for my manners, miss, and any untoward familiarity," he said formally, but almost biting out the words. He was the furthest thing from sorry, I decided. He was convinced I'd tricked him, somehow. And now he looked me between my eyes, not in them. I liked him better when he'd thought me a servant. I wanted to ask why I was 'miss' now, but his scowl was too fierce.

"I'll be on my way there, if it please you?" he said, standing.

"You don't have to please . . . Hugh?" He swayed. Like a young aspen, with those long legs. And his curls shuddered like its leaves do in the slightest breeze. "When did you last eat?" I asked.

His dazed eyes sparked briefly. "Questions. There must be some Celt in you, then?"

His legs gave out from under him, and he fell to his knees. I reached out to steady him, but too late. He tumbled down the incline some twenty or thirty feet, until he landed in Batavia Creek. He wasn't moving. He was facedown in the water's flow.

I slid down the cliff face, and pulled his head from the cold water. He had suffered a bloody gash above the eye. He was pale towards blue, and still.

"Hugh!"

I called his name twice more before his eyelids even flickered. He blinked away the water, then took to coughing again. I helped him sit, then pulled off my red cloak, draping his shaking shoulders. The hacking finally stopped, but the dazed look in his eyes frightened me. Not green eyes, now; they'd turned the slate gray of the creek bed. Changeling eyes he had, like the folk in Mama's fairy books.

"Marcy?" he whispered.

"No, Lily. Lily Woods, remember?"

His eyes went back into his head, and he slumped over, like one of my younger cousins' dancing toys. I felt my mind freezing in panic. Then came splashing steps behind me. I looked up.

"You got you some trouble, Miss Lily?"

I was always happy to see Mr. North. He and his family and community of free colored people lived behind his small blacksmith shop on our side of the clove. Folks still whispered disapproval over my father inviting them to settle among us when the state of New York had declared them free of my Griffin relatives downriver, who'd held them in bondage. But most took advantage of Thomas North's fine workmanship and the washing and cleaning and barber duties his kin took on.

"Is he dead, sir?" I whispered.

Calmly, Mr. North placed the inside of his wrist close to Hugh's mouth. "No," he assured me. "Breathin's regular. The boy's still on God's earth." He smiled. "Your feet's as fleet as a deer's, Miss Lily. Best fetch your granddaddy whilst I look after him, you think?"

"Yes." Both his words and his calmness seemed to be entering my skin, fighting my panic, my numbness. I swaddled Hugh in my cloak.

"I'm going for help," I said at his ear.

The words brought no response, but Mr. North nodded.

I'd never got all the way to my grandparents' cabin on a run before that day. I stood heaving outside the door. Inside I heard the clatter of crockery and my gran's sprightly giggle. There came a lower voice, too, also in good humor. The lavender-colored curtain was pulled across the small front window. I knew what that meant: not to disturb them. Still, I pounded on the door. And I almost kept pounding into my grandfather's billowy shirt as he opened it. He took my hands in that gentle hold of his.

"Breathe easy, Lily, that's the way," he counseled as Gran tucked in his shirt and tied the laces of his trousers behind him. Her hair was undone, here in the middle of the day. They'd been spooning. My parents have a lavender curtain, too. All the married couples in the family do. They have to, with all the children about.

Gran and Daddy Asher stood over me, worry in their eyes. "Are you hurt, child?" Gran asked.

"No. But he is."

"Who?"

"None of ours. A stranger." I sought to clear that worry first. "I didn't know he was sick and teased him into running, and now he's head-bashed and fallen into the creek!"

"You tended him, Lily?"

"Oh, aye, Gran! As best I could. And Mr. North's looking over him now. He's got my cloak. It was all I could think to do once he was out of the water, and breathing."

Daddy Asher looked to Gran. "Put the kettle on, Ginny. We'll return directly."

We were but a foot outside when a bit of russet clothing came flying from the doorway.

"Asher! Your vest!" Gran commanded.

He caught it and, growling, yanked his arms through as we headed toward the embankment. All was accomplished without breaking his sure, barefoot stride.

Now that my grandfather sprinted beside me, my burden lifted further. He smelled of his horses, and a little of Gran's vanilla and berry scent. Asher Woods was a builder—of houses and fields and family and a great line of horses that folks traveled from five states around to buy. He'd survived his ten-year indenture to the Chase family, a Blackfoot raid out west, and a rabid wolf attack in these mountains. Though Gran's Sutherland inheritance had seen that my father and his brothers were formally educated at Harvard and Columbia, truth to tell it was Daddy Asher's wisdom I admired most.

We reached the spot where I'd climbed the cliff. I nodded down to Mr. North and the still figure under my cloak. The blacksmith raised his arm in greeting. My grandfather returned it. Then he took my hand before we slid down the red cliff together.

"Dig your heels, Lily," his quiet voice instructed as he showed me how to slow our descent to the creek bed.

Our dust made the boy turn into the shadow of my cloak and cough. My grandfather knelt and lifted Hugh's head in his big, gentle hands. Daddy Asher's own breath caught in his throat then.

"*Bon Dieu.*" He whispered one of his French blasphemies. "Quinn?"

"Hugh," I corrected. "He said his name is Hugh."

"Hugh Delaney," my grandfather said slowly.

"He didn't say what his—" I stopped when I realized that Hugh's eyelids were flickering open.

"Yes, sir," he murmured as Mr. North transferred his burden to Daddy Asher's strong arms. There between them, Hugh Delaney opened his eyes full. "Begone, Satan!" he yelled at Mr. North. When he saw who held him on the other side, he made a mad struggle to free himself from Daddy Asher. I saw my grandfather with Hugh's eyes then—a towering wilderness Indian savage, his long glossy hair flying back from his shoulders, his high cheekbones and almost pupilless eyes, lightened now, not with color but with mirth.

"Easy," he assured Hugh, "Mr. North ain't the devil. And I'm not going to scalp and eat you any more than I did your kinsman when I held him, years ago."

2

HUGH'S LETTER

Inside my grandparents' cabin, the bedroom door opened. I caught glimpses of my uncle Nathan with his ear at Hugh Delaney's chest. The breeze blew the door shut again.

Daddy Asher, now that he'd seen Mr. North out with a plate of Gran's chicken pie under his arm for his family, sat beside me on the bench in the hall. I looked up. He touched my hair. "Ain't time to worry yet, Lily," he said.

I nodded. "Should I go down to the big house? Tell Mama and Daddy—"

"Mr. North has promised to do that. Stay a while by us. Until we know more."

He turned away, and the shock of silver that ran through his mane of black—a gift of his sparring with the rabid wolf back in the year without a summer—shone in the fading light. Was he afraid? Why did he seek to keep all but our family's healers—the grandmothers and Uncle Nathan—from the Irish boy?

He opened the latest oilcloth-wrapped packages Aunt Tascha and Uncle Reuben had sent from out in the western wilderness. My grandfather was right. What use was it to pass the waiting time in worry? I looked at his bounty and helped him fill the waiting silence with a question.

"Why did the people build these earth mounds, Daddy Asher?"

"Tascha and Reuben think they were burial sites of an ancient people, the ancestors of the Mississippi River Basin Indians."

"Is that what the Indians living there now say?"

"Yes. They call the mound builders 'the old ones.' See?" Daddy Asher's fingers traced along my youngest uncle's words and drawings. "Reuben writes that the other diggers would rather believe they are ancient descendants of people from Egypt or Phoenicia. Even Atlantis." He shook his head. "White people," he said with a sigh of exasperated tolerance. Daddy Asher calls himself Métis for his mixed ancestry, but we both show his Mohican and Wiekagjock line, from our coloring to dark eyes my mother calls "exotically shaped."

"It's good that Reuben and Tascha will write and draw their own account," my grandfather decided.

"Do you wish you were with them, Daddy Asher? Out West again?"

A wistful sadness visited his eyes for only a moment.

"Sometimes," he admitted, then squeezed my knee. "But, were I to join them, who would assure your grandmother that her chicks will come home after their adventure is done? And who would keep her back from the cold over winters in these mountains? And I have a back as well. And my horses and all of you."

I grinned, glad my grandparents still took such delight in each other. And all of us beyond their lavender curtain. "Still, you're lonesome for your away chicks as well," I said.

"Yes. Perhaps I will have to ask our Lily to allow me a place in her adventure to distract me, yes?"

"My adventure?"

He nodded toward the door. "That boy you pulled out of the water. I think maybe he's yours."

"Now, what does that—?"

Uncle Nathan appeared before I could ask about this strange notion. My grandfather stood. Even in his bare feet he was half a head taller than his middle son. I can't remember a single time Daddy Asher lorded his height or strength over any of his five children. "Is it consumption, Nathan?" he asked quietly.

"Now, Daddy, you wouldn't want me making a diagnosis without full consultation with my mentors, would you?" My uncle nodded toward the bedroom door, beyond which my grandmother and great-grandmother were talking softly.

My grandfather smiled. "Not for the world," he admitted.

Uncle Nathan turned to me. He placed his hand along the curve of

my face, resting his thumb at my chin. His touch was warm and soothing, like Gran Constance's. He'd been apprentice to her healing arts
for years before his mama sent him down the Hudson to Columbia
College in New York City to get his physician's degree.

"Everything you and Mr. North did was exactly right, Lily," Uncle
Nathan assured me, before disappearing beyond the door again with
the grandmothers.

But that was not true. I had no business sporting with a boy too sick
to run. We sat. I leaned my head on Daddy Asher's arm. "Is consumption a bad disease?" I asked.

"It is."

"You've seen it before," I realized as I said the words.

"My brother died of it."

"Out West? In your trapping days?"

He nodded, then sat very still, even for my grandfather, who fits in
without a seam in the silences of our forests. I knew which brother he
meant then, the one who had survived the Blackfoot raid but not the
winter they hid out together in a cave. That brother was the one that
his first son, my daddy, was named for—Joshua.

"Is consumption catching?" I whispered.

"I caught it."

I didn't know that part of the story. "Is that why you've forbidden
my mama and daddy to come up here? Because it's a catching sickness?"

"Yes. I'll have to send all away, if the boy's still coughing blood."

"What about you?"

He shrugged. "I don't expect I'll catch it again."

I hugged his arm.

"He comes from good stock, this boy," Daddy Asher claimed, his
voice warming a little. "Quinn was in terrible shape there on the battlefield at Plattsburgh in '14. Nobody thought he'd last the day. But he
did. He still had ten years in him. And his mother survived him long
enough to dote on you, Lily."

I knew the stories of how Mrs. Delaney had stayed on with us after
her soldier son died. How she became part of our household, helping
Gran birth her last baby, Aunt Tascha, twenty-five years ago. Mrs. Delaney provided assistance in all the birthings of the generation that followed soon after, too.

But our friend was never more joyful than at my arrival into the family, everyone says. I came when my parents were married seven years and my father had contented himself with the love of Mama and Jane, Mama's daughter by her first husband, Alexander McKay. By the time Mama found she was to be a mother again, my half sister was almost as old as I am now. As a surprise child, I was doted upon by all, they say, but none more than Mrs. Delaney.

I have fond remembrances of Mrs. Delaney—a round, smiling face and floury hands, fireside stories of saints and sinners, and heroes and wolves. The big house is so empty without her. I was a carrying-on child, Mrs. Delaney used to say. And when I asked her of what, she'd say, "Of what you listen so well to, child. Stories. And stories are life." I leaned again on my grandfather's bony but somehow comfortable shoulder. What was Hugh Delaney's story?

"I wonder who Marcy is?" I whispered, like a sigh.

"Marcy?"

"It's who Hugh thought I was, there by the creek, before he went frail."

"How did he look at you?"

"Happy. For a moment. Then frightened."

Daddy Asher winced, glancing toward the bedroom door. "She's dead, his Marcy, I suspect."

He knew more about death than the rest of us put together. Before his brother Joshua died of consumption, Daddy Asher had lost his whole birth family—father, mother, brothers and baby sister—in the Blackfoot raid. Ten years after, he was captain in the volunteer militia in the Second War of Independence. He fought in the Battle of Plattsburgh when the creeks ran red with blood. If my grandfather thought Hugh's Marcy was dead, I was sure of it.

The door opened as Gran and Gran Constance, followed by Uncle Nathan, slipped through. I got a little longer glimpse inside this time. Hugh lay still, his pale face framed by the coal-black curls plastered to it. The room was steamy, infused with the restorative scent of Saint-John's-wort.

"We're agreed," Uncle Nathan spoke for himself, Gran, and Gran Constance as he closed the door. "The boy's in weak health, but over his coughing sickness, which was more likely pneumonia than consumption."

"And his fall?" I asked. "His head?"

"A good, hard head," my great-grandmother assured me. "He'll suffer little more than a bruise, I expect."

Gran Constance gave Uncle Nathan her pitcher. I was pleased with not only their pronouncement but the slow, measured way they spoke it. Both had a habit of using short, staccato sentences when they were worried.

Gran smiled. "Come eat, rescuers," she said.

We followed Uncle Nathan and the graceful glide of the two women's skirts into the hearth room. The men talked about horses as I helped Gran and Gran Constance prepare a tea for us all.

As I was setting the table I found Gran's favorite rose-colored hair ribbon under a Windsor chair. Gran Constance took it from my hand. Then she made her daughter sit long enough to allow her to wind it among her braids.

Daddy Asher stopped talking with Uncle Nathan long enough to admire the women in that square of late afternoon sunshine. His eyes shone with something that turned beyond admiration, I thought. It was as if he'd been watching them in those same hairdressing gestures since Gran was a girl at her mama's knee. Which he had, I realized, as they'd been lifelong neighbors most of his sixty-two years. Gran tried to bolt from Gran Constance's hold before her tie was complete.

"Mind your mama, Ginny Rockwell," he chided her, grinning.

"There," Gran Constance declared when her daughter was beribboned to her satisfaction. Gran realized we were all admiring her mother's skill and her own beauty, and she blushed deeply. When I look at my mother and grandmothers, I look forward to the life ahead of me.

"Would you pour, Lily?" Gran asked as she brought the teapot to the table. She knew I needed the practice for the more formal times Mama asked me to perform hostess duties at the big house. And she knew I had failed miserably learning these things over the months at Mrs. Beech's boarding school. I nodded, though I would never feel at ease in our dining room as I did at the grans' hearth. I was grateful that my grandfather and Uncle Nathan took their China tea black, so I didn't have to shave sugar and pour cream for them.

I knew to ask no questions until my duties at table were complete. I was careful to add the half spoon of sugar for Gran Constance and the heaping one for Gran. We were all taking bites of Gran's luscious raspberry tarts bathed in vanilla sauce when Uncle Nathan finally spoke of the boy in Aunt Tascha's bed.

"It was hard to get a word out of him after I listened to his lungs, mentioned consumption," he told us. "It took the womenfolk to calm down his ire once I suggested he'd brought a communicative disease to our valley. He railed as much as his diminished strength would allow! 'How would I have got through the port of New York? Do you think those rough men who poked and prodded me wouldn't have sent me home?' " My uncle shook his head. "The boy's full of questions, isn't he?"

I asked my own question then. "Did he say 'me' and not 'us,' Uncle Nathan?"

"I believe so, Lily."

His Marcy was dead before they had reached New York, then. "Will he recover his health?" I asked.

"If he stops pretending he's hearty and gets what he needs," Gran started.

"Rest, fresh food to fill him out again," Uncle Nathan agreed.

"Care." Gran Constance mused, shaking her head. "Boys are so heedless in their own care, especially one with so much anger in him." She eyed Daddy Asher until he stopped watching the breeze waft through the loose-weave curtain. "Are they not, Asher Woods?"

He smiled with half his face. "I have long ceased dare to debate your observations of human nature, madame," he said.

"Where are his folks, Asher?" Gran asked.

Daddy Asher grunted his displeasure. "That child's not talking to me until he's convinced I won't open his skull with a tomahawk," he said. With a gentle look Gran softened his mood before he continued. "Mrs. Delaney used to write to folks in Ireland, didn't she? The woman who sent her the black lace shawl after Quinn died. Remember, Ginny?" He enlisted Gran's help in the puzzle that was Hugh Delaney.

"That's right. Cousins?"

"Yes," Daddy Asher affirmed, "that's how I remember it."

"Mrs. Delaney received letters, too. At Christmastime, for a few years, then nothing," Gran continued. "But she never stopped writing. We posted the letters together." She closed her eyes in concentration.

"I thought they were churchmen, because part of the address was an abbey . . . yes, in a pretty-sounding place—Roscommon. Mrs. Delaney laughed and said they were farmers and artisans, from a place that was named for a long-ago abbey. My, how it does come back to me." She looked startled by her own recollection. "There'd be more to it in Mrs. Delaney's trunk. That's still in her room in the big house, I believe."

"And you think Hugh Delaney looks like Quinn?" Uncle Nathan asked Daddy Asher.

"Don't you, son?"

"I was only ten when Quinn died, Daddy," he replied, with some hesitation in his voice, I thought. "Perhaps Susannah and Josh would remember better."

"No. No, they wouldn't," Daddy Asher said. "Hugh looks like Quinn, but before."

"Before?" I prompted.

"When I found him on the battlefield, Lily, he was a boy, like this one. His wounds, they took their toll on him. By the time we visited the Delaneys in Albany, even Josh didn't believe Quinn was younger than me."

"He was so gray and frail, Daddy," Uncle Nathan agreed.

My grandfather looked over the mantel where the rifle the government had gifted to him for his service was mounted. "I never saw him that way. To me, he was just Quinn."

That was the way it was for my grandfather, our Mrs. Delaney had often explained to me. Once a person became his friend, all other distinctions that others saw or deemed important melted. Quinn, who was enemy and Irish and Catholic and crippled and sick, became just Quinn.

Daddy Asher turned back to his son. "Nathan. It's like he's come again."

Gran laid her hand over Daddy Asher's.

"Well. That's good enough for me," Uncle Nathan said. He reached between his shirt and vest pocket. "The boy asked me to deliver this to you, Daddy. That is, if you are really Asher Woods of whom his cousin wrote and not a . . . now, how did he put it, it was so picturesque . . . 'fiend from the American wilderness that not even the archangel Michael might vanquish.' "

He handed his father a paper that was folded almost to shreds.

Daddy Asher stared at his son. "What were *you* waiting for? For me to prove myself in league with God?"

"No, Daddy!" Uncle Nathan laughed. "For Hugh Delaney to prove himself. They are teeming into the port of New York, the Irish, since the potato blight over there in recent years has caused a great famine. Many come with false recommendations, promises of work, in order to gain entrance to America. I needed to hear your recollections to assure myself he could be who he says he is, a relative of our Mrs. Delaney."

Daddy Asher shook his head. "I thought only the lawyer children were so suspicious, Ginny." He passed the paper to his wife. "Here, try out your new spectacles."

Gran reached into her apron's deep pockets and drew out the box Hugh and I had fought over. She brought forth her gleaming, steel-rimmed spectacles and placed them across the bridge of her nose. They fit well, but that's not what caused her bright smile. "This is Mrs. Delaney's hand," she announced.

"Good. Excellent. Read it, Mama," Uncle Nathan urged.

"It's dated October 23, 1849."

"Almost two years ago," I said.

"And scarcely a month before our Mrs. Delaney died of that sudden brain fever," Gran added. "She was hale and hearty until the very end, remember, Lily?"

I nodded.

"I wonder if she somehow knew her time was growing short?" Gran said. She looked again at the fragile paper. "Well, let's see what she writes.

"My dear Cousin Eavan,

"It is with great sadness I learned of you left without your husband. Christy was a worthy son of Bran, a brother who my husband spoke of with a great affection.

"This draught is good for funds in the bank where the others have come through. Please God it will make your and the children's winter a brighter one, as mine have been since first I came to this new country of America. Still, I long to see the rising mists off the Arigna Mountains. Tell me of them, will you, dear? Then I might pass the images on to the Woods children, with whom God in his goodness has never ceased to indulge me since my Quinn's passing. Of late, I think I hear O'Carolan's melodies wafting about these American peaks, calling me home. Imagine that?

"If you have fallen upon hard times, do get word to me, dear. I would do whatever is in my power to protect my husband's kin from harm. You wrote of the landlord's putting more hardship on your family. You feared losing acres held by the family from the time of the High Kings.

"Such things would not happen here in America, cousin. Though the soil of these mountains is not so yielding as the land of our birth, it is owned freely, and no longer by the whims or greed of landlords. Young men cannot be yanked from their beds and impressed into the wars here, as my Quinn was.

"It was soon after I lost my husband and felt sure my son would follow, a casualty of the war with America, that Captain Woods, my son's sworn enemy, called to me. My feelings at that moment no human tongue can tell. Imagine me holding the notice from the British that told of my son's death, and the letter from America saying no, he was wounded and secreted away. This man, Quinn's enemy, offered his remaining life to my care. Which should I believe? The British who had stolen my fine young son? Or the captain of the savage Americans who'd shot him down in the bloom of his youth?

"I chose to be with my son, even if we were to become prisoners of the Americans. It proved a good choice, Eavan. My ten years with Quinn held more blessings than I can describe. More surprising still has been this time after his passing. They who sustain me are uncommon, even in this uncommon country. They who I called my enemies have welcomed me so that I have never felt in their service, but as one of their own, even as the infirmities of my advanced age have me less useful to them and their flocks of little ones.

"God Himself would be hard-pressed to find a better family that walks the earth these days than the one headed by Captain Asher Woods and his lady. It is in knowing this that I make bold enough to tell you that they would turn away none of my family who came to them in a time of need. Let this be the record of your welcome. Bring it and your dear selves to Stony Clove, up the Hudson River in the northernmost Catskill Mountains of New York State, should the times ever warrant it. You will not be lost, whether I'm here to greet you or no, while any here remembers me.

Your loving cousin,
Connel Delaney."

"Connel," Gran repeated, pulling off her spectacles to dab at eyes now wet with tears. "I never thought to ask Mrs. Delaney's Christian name. Lovely. It suits her."

"I'll carve it into her stone," Daddy Asher said, touching her shoulder. "Would that please you, Ginny?"

"It would, love," she assured him, as if he were the one weeping.

Mrs. Delaney and her son were buried among the Sutherlands, the folks who owned the place before us. It's been our family graveyard since Gran was given the estate by Squire Sutherland when she reached her majority almost forty years ago. But none of ours is yet buried there, a fact that some envious people of Stony Clove find strange. I'd not thought much about it. It gave me a chill suddenly, now. Had we been, unlike those starving Irish and massacred members of Asher Woods's long-gone family, too fortunate?

"Well, young Hugh is surely Quinn's cousin," Uncle Nathan said, dispelling my gloom. "But we'd best get him located away from here, what with—"

"Not before I've filled him out some," Gran insisted. "I have all of Mrs. Delaney's favorite meals written out."

"You will be due for some deliveries, will you not, Mama?" Nathan asked her pointedly. "Daddy?" he looked to his father, whose eyes had wandered back to the curtains and his mind back to the past, I thought.

"Most likely, what with this new law," Daddy Asher answered his middle son softly. "But let Hugh stay a little while."

"We must be careful," Nathan warned. "Delaney or not, this boy is a stranger. Up from New York City, where there is no love between the Irish and the colored people who compete for the same jobs, and fiercely."

"And you are still a heedless boy, Asher Woods," Gran Constance scolded. She'd taken Uncle Nathan's side against Daddy Asher. But why their argument took in the subject of colored people and a new law, I could only speculate.

"Are you expecting a painting shipment, Gran?" I asked, as I knew her youngest brother, Charlie, who ministers to an immigrant congregation on Manhattan's West Side, occasionally brought her purchased works of art by steamship up the Hudson.

"Your grandmother and her projects," Daddy Asher said with a grumble, but not matching his eyes to mine. Hiding. Because there was no dissembling in him. I'd heard both grans say that often enough to know it. "I need to tend the horses," he said, abruptly heading for the door. "Coming, Nathan?"

"Glad to help, Daddy. Then I promised Pen to stop for a pint of syrup," Uncle Nathan claimed, following. "I'll check our patient at first light, Mama, Gran," he promised. Both men left their plates with ample portions of their tarts uneaten.

That was not like either, despite Daddy Asher's love of horses and Nathan's for Aunt Pen, whom he had brought home from New York City years ago along with his doctor's degree. Aunt Pen is dark and beautiful and called the Gypsy by those who envy their affection. They have two babies now, Albert and Eliza, and they live in town. Aunt Pen's sister, Beatrice, still lives in New York City, married to our minister uncle, Charlie Steenwyck—who was, perhaps, sending more than paintings up the river to my grandmother.

My grandmothers stared daggers at the men's backs. Then they busied themselves searching out Gran's book of Mrs. Delaney's recipes, talking over each other's sentences before I fisted my hands at my waist and stared them down. "Don't worry. I'll ask no more about your shipments, Gran," I assured both. "Or the law that causes more in number."

They both looked stunned. There. I'd finally let them know I had at least an inkling of my family's secret business. When would they allow me knowledge of it?

3

JANE'S SCHOOL

When my mother opened the door to my bedroom, she let in the night breeze from the hallway. With it came the sound of my father and grandfather's argument downstairs.

"She could be safe at Mrs. Beech's school now!" my father shouted at his.

"Safe? Amid stiff-necked people calling her a savage?"

"Daddy. No one called her—"

"Not to her face, of course! But our Lily has all the wit that you and Sarah possess, Josh. Do you think any of their artifice was lost on her? Do you value that kind of place and its safety over your daughter's happiness?"

"She's a child! What does she know about what will make her happy?"

"She knows enough to pull a sick boy from the creek, to—"

"To open herself to catching his sickness—"

Uncle Nathan's patient voice sounded between their warring ones. "As I told you both, the danger of infection is past. Do return to existing issues."

"May I take out your braid tonight, Lily?" my mother asked, closing the door and muffling their voices.

As much as I wanted to ask her why she wasn't downstairs helping Uncle Nathan, acting her usual mediator role between my father and his, I remained silent. She seemed too fragile as she sat beside me on the bench, her full, deep green skirts forming a perfect whirling pattern out from her waist. She let out my heavy flaxen braid with fingers that gradually became more sure, familiar. By the time she began brushing my hair back off my brow, I closed my eyes to the comfort of her strokes.

The arguments between the two men I loved best in the world disturbed me, even when I was not their cause. They'd been going on long before I was born, the women of the family assured me, and were bound to happen between two men as disparate as Daddy Asher and his eldest son. Their disagreements concerned only the means by which family goals were accomplished, never the ends, my aunt Susannah, Daddy's twin, once assured me. Still, I thought they should try harder to understand each other, as there was enough dissension among my two families on either side of the Hudson.

Even though Mama was from a distant Scottish branch of the Griffins, they had sponsored her trip to America when she was an impoverished young widow with six-year-old Jane depending on her to make a good match for her second husband. Daddy, barely twenty and the son of the Griffins' enemy Asher Woods, was not the man they had in mind. But he'd swept Mama out of their clutches before they realized they'd lost her.

The Griffins did not even correspond with Mama in the early years of their marriage, when Daddy still took old roosters as tender for his fees. But then his country lawyer's place in the world began to rise. He was named town clerk, then circuit judge, then court justice. The Griffins reestablished their contact with congratulations upon my birth. My father sometimes complains they caught Mama and him in a generous mood. One thing is certain: Mama is caught, as I am, on a bridge between the two families, which are as unlike each other as can be imagined.

"I wonder if your hair will darken to your father's brown," she mused. "Mother Ginny tells me his was almost as gold as yours when he was a child. It will become you either way, if it remains so lustrous and healthy. This family—it's delightful, seeing how the babies come out!"

Others thought our blood mix strange—servants with freeborn, Yankee New Englanders with Dutch, French Huguenots with Wiekagjock and Mohican, down to my father's combination of all of these with a Scotswoman from the Isle of Skye. But my mother always called it our strength, our "American spirit," manifesting itself in diverse passions—for justice, science, equality, democracy, the arts, and husbandry of the land. But laced through us was a quiet tolerance, she claimed, since so many diverse people's blood ran in our veins.

It was not considered a strength at Mrs. Beech's school. Neither was the tone of my skin, brought on, Mrs. Beech herself insisted, from my habit of wearing hats with brims not wide enough to protect me from the sun's damage. I was not damaged, only related to people of a scorned race. Daddy Asher was right about that place. There, my teachers said my heritage was the reason I had no social graces and accounted for a "streak of wildness" that might prove impossible to combat. How did embroidery hoops and tea services and stiff corsets combat anything? Or hadn't I tried hard enough in my aching, homesick months there? Why had my own sister insisted I go?

"I can't wait to see the next generation," Mama said, beginning a loose night braid down my back. She doted on babies and children. When Jane had turned twenty-nine, she informed us that she had no interest in marriage and mothering, only her school, reforms, and the abolition of slavery. I was shy and awkward, still thought of as a child despite being in reach of sixteen—the age when Gran had married Daddy Asher. I had no admirers, and I'd frustrated all attempts of my teachers to make me a proper young lady. No babies from me seemed likely in the near future. Poor Mama.

"Are you greatly disappointed that I asked to come home from school?" I asked her.

"Why, Lily, of course not. There was much consternation about allowing you to go in the first place, remember?"

I remembered the same two voices raised downstairs over that family issue, with my sister's voice holding sway in their deadlock.

"Your grandfather has not gloated, bless him," Mama said. "He was quite correct—how could a finishing school compare with your grandmother's library, and all that this family and these mountains have taught you? But, Lily, there are no Harvards, no Princetons or Columbias for us women. Our higher learning concentrates itself on household management and social graces. And your disposition is sweeter, less blunt than Jane's, Lily."

"It is?"

"Aye. She thought if you took to some of Mrs. Beech's precepts . . . well, I think our Jane saw you winning battles that she cannot in the community and at her school."

What was impossible for my sister to accomplish?

"You will forgive your sister, won't you, Lily?" Mama asked uneasily.

"Forgive her? Whatever for?"

"For the suggestion . . . no, Jane never suggests. For the command that you attempt Mrs. Beecher's school. She's written me, sure you're angry. She thinks that's why you haven't visited or thought about taking a teaching situation there."

"I only just arrived home! And I am already disappointing her," I admitted. "The students she's left in my care here are leaving my instruction in droves."

"That's the harvest coming in, Lily."

"More because I'm not Jane."

"Oh, love." My beautiful mother shook her head sadly.

Downstairs, the heavy front door slammed shut. We both rushed to my window to see Uncle Nathan mount his horse and ride off. He'd either succeeded or given up. Or remembered his promise to Aunt Pen again. We returned to the dressing table, where Mama put down my brush. Daddy's and my grandfather's argument resumed as she lifted back the covers of my bed the way she had when I was younger. I climbed between the creamy sheets, and she sat beside me.

"Lily, do you remember the nights your father was away for weeks on the circuit court and the three of us—you and Jane and I—used to climb into the big bed and read the books of French fairy tales?"

"Yes, Mama."

The voices downstairs became louder. French phrases from his trapper days were exploding from Daddy Asher. He was not reciting fairy tales. He was blaspheming.

"Don't you want to go downstairs, Mama?" I asked nervously. "To intercede?"

"Your father," she began, and I heard the frown in her voice, "should know by this time that your grandparents would turn away none in need, were he from Ireland, the Carolinas, or Kathmandu! And Daddy Asher should be more mindful of my husband's position in town and the state judiciary and among my relatives. Oh, Lily, I am so out of patience with them both!" she declared firmly.

"Hugh is Mrs. Delaney's kin, Mama," I said. "And I am sure he'll cause no one trouble once he's well."

"He has come to a country he knows little about, I suspect. A country in turmoil. Still, there is the free-labor cotton mill, and the tanning factories, and the little Catholic chapel upon the hill. Perhaps those will bring him comfort."

"They are more than what you had, Mama."

"Ah, but I had your father's bright and shining passion for me, for my Jane. And I had this family."

I thought of Daddy Asher's words about Quinn Delaney's kin. "Hugh will have our family, too, won't he?"

"I expect so, yes."

"Why don't you go down and tell them this?" I urged.

"Oh, Lily. The Irish boy might have been the spark, but neither he nor you is the real source of their argument."

"He isn't?"

"No. I expect Mrs. Delaney's cousin will do well for himself, if he is anything like that fine lady. They now argue about my trip downriver, I think."

"Downriver?"

"Yes. At first light."

"Are you going to visit Jane, Mama?"

She kissed my cheek. "Yes."

"At her school?"

"There is no school anymore, darling. It burned to the ground. The telegraph rider just brought the news of it out of Catskill."

I felt a terrible pounding start inside my head. I reached out blindly, as if I were a child in the dark. My mother took me into her arms. It did not feel as safe there as when I was a child, for she was shaking.

"I was supposed to be there," I whispered. "Jane said to come, to help her, if I would not stay at the boarding school."

"But you missed our mountains. It would not do to pack you off downriver so soon." My mother stroked my hair with fingers that trembled anew. "Thank all that's holy you were not there. I might have lost you both."

"Mama! Is Jane—"

"Jane is safe at Locust Haven. My aunt, the Widow Webber, wired that—"

"The Widow? What's wrong? Why doesn't Jane send word herself?"

"She's recovering."

"Recovering?"

"Her hands and arms were burned as a result of her efforts to help the young ladies flee."

"Oh, Mama, were any—"

"I know no more than that from my aunt's message. But the widow has agreed to allow Jane's students to stay in the old slave quarters at Locust Haven, until their sponsors can return them to their families or suitable positions in Boston or New York."

"That was good of the Widow Webber, wasn't it?" I said in surprise. Our downriver relatives judged my sister Jane's School for Ladies and Misses of Color a personal affront, as did most in their town on the other side of the Hudson's banks.

"Yes. I am indebted to my aunt's generosity. And that is more the reason for the argument between your father and grandfather downstairs, I suspect. They worry about what toll the Widow Webber's generosity will take on this family. But I am a Griffin, so she is my family, too. They are both too volatile, these men. I will brook none of it. Your uncle Nathan is more sensible. He has agreed to accompany me tomorrow. While Asher and Joshua Woods continue their arguments, we will do what's of first importance—bring our Jane home."

"Might I come, Mama?"

"No, Lily. You must see that your father keeps his attention on his court duties. Complete your teaching, before all your charges are sprung for the harvest. And help your grandmothers with this poor Irish boy who has entered our family at a most tumultuous time."

"Might you manage all that, darling Lily?" my father whispered from the doorway. He looked worn out, but so handsome in his finely cut frock coat, his chest braced by his snowy shirt and black satin cravat and a waistcoat of the swirling colors of our mountains in autumn. It was the new Justice Joshua Woods who stood there in his matching butternut-brown suit. But it was my father, too, boyish despite his forty-one years, even as he bowed formally, hoping for what he immediately received: Mama's forgiveness and an invitation into our circle. He climbed into the bed and hugged us both, burying his face in Mama's lustrous red hair.

"We will weather this, won't we, Sarah?" he asked her.

Mama pulled him closer, nodding.

"There. I am the richest man on earth," he whispered.

4

HUGH'S DREAM

It was almost dawn when I ran up the hill beyond our house to Gran's place to see how Hugh was faring. Gran met me at the door, her long braid over her shoulder, its ends almost touching the waistband of her apron. Her fingers bore dark brown stains, so I knew what she'd been up to.

"Counting your gold, Dragon?" I asked.

"Indeed!"

She laughed, knowing I'd come upon her early-morning task of writing in the cream-colored pages of her journals. Traders or housekeepers who'd caught her in the same position had spread word of Ginny Rockwell the dragon. She was always counting money, some folks held, or figuring what to invest her great fortune in, be it railroad or textile or steamship company. When first I told Gran this, she replied, "I can barely stand talking on that subject twice a year with your father and my brothers!" But "Ginny Rockwell, the gold-hoarding dragon" has been a jest between us ever since.

And it felt good this morning, with my mother gone to fetch Jane home and my father presiding over his new court duties, to sit in this place as loved and familiar as my own home, twirling Gran's goose quills as I watched her sprinkle pounce on the latest beautiful strokes in the book Daddy Asher had bound for her. Though ink is now bottled by chemists, Gran still makes her own from oak and chestnut galls. She owns an elegant inkstand, though, that includes two inkwells, a pounce box, quill holder, penknife and wiper, an erasing knife, and a taperstick to hold a small candle for melting sealing wax. It even has a little bell for summoning a servant to deliver a letter, which Daddy Asher says is for him, though I've never heard it ring.

I glanced toward the hall beyond the hearth room. Gran followed my gaze with a knowing smile. "I'll ladle out a portion from the pot of Mrs. Delaney's porridge, if you'll see if that other gift she's lately left us is stirring."

"Did he sleep well, Gran?"

"Almost straight through the night."

"Almost?"

"There's still some coughing left in him, poor boy. Asher and I took turns propping him higher, soothing his heaves with maple sugar tea. Neither my early morning scratching nor your grandfather's ramble up to his sweat lodge have caused more than a sigh from our new chick." Gran sighed a small sigh herself. "It's a sweet thing, having that bed filled again."

She seemed to cast herself into a dream. About her away children, no doubt. When her eyes become like that I know I come by the same tendency honestly. "Go on," Gran said, seeming surprised I was still there. "Maybe the oats will bring him 'round."

Gran was right. Hugh's first word when he opened his eyes was, "Porridge?"

"There, the scent has given you a little color." I laughed. But his face stayed sober and worried as he stared at my steaming bounty.

"I don't have any money, miss," he whispered.

"You don't need any here."

"Nothing's to be had in America without money."

"Is that the way it's been for you, Hugh?"

Gran put her head in the doorway. "Lily Woods, pour his tea and allow the boy to eat," she chided. "Then would you scout out your grandfather? Tell him there's a hungry boy sharing his breakfast today. That should get him into the world of the practical fast enough."

Blossoms on Gran's pea vines and lilac bushes soon were replaced by early wildflowers. They wove a path to Daddy Asher's steaming sweat lodge. The small framework of bark-covered branches stood not far from the field of wild strawberries this year. Their flowers are among the first to show after our hard winters. I could tell from tracks wet from his dive in the lake and the open flaps of the lodge that my grandfather was making ready to begin his day.

Beyond the structure, the path that led over Second Sister Mountain was widened and fresh cut. As I was puzzling that over in my mind, I felt a hand on my shoulder. When I did not startle at Daddy Asher's touch, he spun me around and looked crestfallen.

"You heard my approach, Lily."

"Only the last three footfalls!"

He grunted, turning away. "It's a good thing Ginny Rockwell never had a great taste for fresh meat."

"Daddy says you are the best tracker he's ever seen."

"Your father is a Boston lawyer turned sit-down judge. That's hardly high praise."

"Are you still angry with him, Grandfather?" I addressed him formally in my worry.

His laughing eyes sobered, but he did not speak.

"You've sweated in your lodge since before dawn," I coaxed, "after sitting up with Hugh last night. And Gran is writing in her book." I backed away from him, confused by my own conflicting emotions.

"Lily," he called, holding out his arms, "we do not mean to burden you."

I nodded, first stopping my retreat, then rushing into his embrace. I buried my head in the familiar feel of his hard-muscled chest and the balsam scent that made my mother call him Father Christmas. I thought of Mama gone to fetch Jane home, and the boy in Tascha's bed, as my tears soaked the homespun of Daddy Asher's shirt.

He shook his head. "We are all of us a stubborn people, Lily. That's part of why we hold on to this place we love. We have a duty to this land, and to each other. We disagree sometimes, on the particulars, that's all. Your father and I, we argued. But our anger dissolves like morning mist."

I buried my head deeper.

"Does it not?" he tried. "Mostly?"

I came up long enough to look at him, and was so dismayed by his forlorn expression that I had to smile. "Mostly," I agreed.

We ducked into his sweat lodge, where Daddy Asher fetched up his medicine bag, tying its strings around the brace of his trousers. I liked the scent of steam and sage that still permeated the place. Daddy

Asher's medicine bag and sweat lodge were two of the reasons some folks in town still called him a heathen savage who should have stayed in the western wilderness where he sought his birth family. Only Ginny Rockwell's money protected him from the town's censure, they maintained. Did Daddy Asher ever care what folks like that thought of him? He gave no evidence of it for as long as my memory spans.

I faced my grandfather through the steamy warmth of the lodge. "Did you throw your stones, Daddy Asher?" I asked him.

"Yes."

"Why?"

"Because of a dream."

"What did you dream?"

"Not my dream. The one that woke the boy."

"Hugh? In the night?"

"Yes."

"He told you his dream?"

"Yes. Imagine that?" He grinned as we both remembered Hugh's initial reaction to finding himself in Daddy Asher's arms. "I think maybe Sally Hamilton browbeat him into it."

"Sally Hamilton? He saw our ghost in his dream?"

"I think so. On the water. She waited for him in her trim little sloop. She told him to hand over passengers, he said."

"Passengers?"

"Thirteen. Women and children. Shrouded in smoke, and the night around them, without the moon or stars for guidance."

"Did he hand them over?"

"Started to. Then saw someone else."

"Marcy."

"Marcella, yes. His sister, lately dead. The one he took you for, Lily. That's when he ran, with the ferrywoman calling after him."

"Poor Hugh."

My grandfather agreed, nodding. "I tried to explain how he'd best listen to Sally Hamilton, do as she bids him, once we figure out who the thirteen are and how to get them on board."

I pictured my grandfather doing exactly that, in the same voice he'd use instructing him on the care of horses or the planting of corn. "Did he think you mad, Daddy Asher?"

"Not then, at least. Maybe with the light of day he will, yes? But

Mrs. Delaney was not run on an excess of reason. Neither was Quinn, for all his book learning. *The boy comes from good stock, open to possibilities. But he had the dream here, Lily. The stones say to keep him close, to give him our trust. In that your father and I differ. Among other things.*" A fresh morning breeze swept through the opened flaps of the lodge, replacing the sage scent with one of lilacs. "I'm hungry," Daddy Asher declared suddenly. "Had breakfast?"

"That's why I'm sent to fetch you home."

"And your grandmother's doting on that scrawny boy. We could starve. Best race."

He only waited until I had kilted up my skirts before he tore down the trail beside me. He never forged ahead, though I'm sure he could have. Asher Woods has won races against men half his age at Fourth of July town festivals. He's supposed to march his militiamen then, too, on the village green before the fireworks, but he frolics with them and their children and grandchildren instead.

Why are you opening the trail over Second Sister, Daddy Asher?" I asked him at our breakfast table.

A quick glance passed between him and Gran on the other side of me.

"Maybe I'm tired of your grandmother and her capital ventures in railroads and free-labor cotton mills. Maybe I'm going to open an excursion business for the tourists so they can experience the vistas from Second Sister in comfort of limb and delight to eyes."

"And maybe the moon will turn green!" I scoffed.

"Why, Lily." He opened his eyes wide in mock surprise. "You cut me to the quick!"

"Seriously," I pleaded. When he avoided my eyes, I turned to Gran.

"Seriously," she said, as that look passed between them again. "The younger grandchildren would like to pick blueberries with me this summer up there."

"And?"

Her eyes caught sight of her walking stick by the fireplace. "And your grandfather thinks me quite incapable of carrying my own grandbabies!"

"Just on the last, steepest slope, Ginny," Daddy Asher insisted, forking through seven layers of buckwheat cakes and swallowing them down with satisfaction. "Use your stick coming back from the Tinkors' place," he added for good measure.

"Impossible man," she scolded him.

"Why are you going to the Tinkors', Gran?"

Daddy Asher snorted, and took a drink of his chickory root coffee. "Seems our guest is used to honey with his cream and porridge, if you please."

"Why, Gran—"

"I'm in need of a good walk to sharpen my wits maybe, as long as I have a husband who orders me about and answers all questions on my behalf!" she shot back at him.

Daddy Asher held up his hand. "Peace, woman," he asked, half in jest, I thought, for he liked sparring with his wife.

Once my grandfather headed out for his horses, Gran went on talking about berries and bears and the growing limbs of their grandchildren as we finished clearing the table. Then she sent me to collect our guest's breakfast remains.

I found Hugh Delaney standing by the window of Aunt Tascha's room, watching Daddy Asher in the ring with Little Coy.

"Do you ride?" I asked quietly.

Hugh started, then scrambled back into the bed. His cheeks were flaming with embarrassment, but I didn't know if it stemmed from my seeing him in Uncle Reuben's nightclothes or being caught up on his feet.

"Beg pardon, miss," he grumbled, more a complaint than an apology.

"For what?"

"I didn't hear you come in." His changeable eyes went frightened. "Why didn't I hear you?"

"Are your ears still crackling?"

"Who told you—"

"My uncle Nathan. He says it's natural at our altitude and with you recovering."

"Will he come back, the doctor?"

"Not for a while. But my grandmothers will take good care of you. Uncle Nathan's gone downriver with my mother, to treat my sister Jane."

"The schoolmistress? The one who's burned?"

"Yes. You have been talking with someone."

"The *bean-a-tighe*." At my quizzical expression, his cheeks flamed again. "Lady of the house," he translated. "Ginny Rockwell—that is to say, Mrs. Woods. She told me. I am sorry for your trouble."

There. He was giving me a measure of sympathy. "And I'm sorry for the loss of your sister Marcella," I said.

His head went down so far I could see only the spiraling start of his wild curls. "Who told you of Marcy?" he whispered.

"My grandfather. He was there when you cried out from your dream, remember?"

His head lifted. "That wasn't a dream as well?"

"No."

"He must think me a fool."

"Oh, no. He respects dreams. And loss. And the ferrywoman you saw? She's our family's ghost."

"What are you saying, now?"

"Well, we think of her that way, though we inherited her from Squire Sutherland. She was his servant, and he caused her death, back in colony days. Daddy Asher's seen her since he was a boy and she was still haunting the Squire. She's adopted us since, I think. The grans say they sense her about at birthing times. Helping out. And she even came to my father once, when he was my age, and Daddy Asher was dying from a rabid wolf's bite! Maybe he won Daddy Asher back from death for us, my aunt Susannah says. But you mustn't tell anyone that. Daddy's very respectable."

"That's why his family lives in the big, respectable house?"

"Exactly so! He fits better than the rest of us, and he's always loved the house best, so we keep it for parties, and the library. Gran has the most wonderful art gallery collected there, one that we open to the public three days a week. But the house is a trial for Mama and me to keep up after your cousin's passing." I was talking too much, as I'm wont to do when the subject is family. And Hugh's eyes looked pained. "Daddy Asher lost a sister, too. A baby. She was murdered out West. My aunt Susannah's named for her. She's my father's twin."

Hugh's head bowed again, though perhaps not so low. "I didn't take good enough care of my sister. On the boat. She never saw America. She died of the coughing, and they . . . they dropped her into that cold water."

I touched one white-knuckled finger.

"I carried on, like I promised her. Couldn't find work, though."

"You'll find what you need here, Hugh."

His grip eased.

"Is there any more of your family down in New York?" I asked. "Or across the water in Ireland? I'm sure Gran—"

"She's already asked me. I'm the last."

"Like Daddy Asher was the last of his folks, when he came back here. I'm sorry, Hugh. I'm so sorry."

"Thank you, miss." He reached up to where the edge of his cap would have been, and tugged at his forelock.

I sighed at his formality. "How old are you?" I asked.

"Seventeen, miss."

"Well, I'm fifteen. Would you call me Lily, so I'm not required to 'mister' you back?"

"I would not expect—"

"Daddy Asher would. And might accuse me of putting on airs, if I allowed your 'miss' while I call you by your Christian name." I nodded toward the window. "You wouldn't want me to get out of his good graces, would you?"

He grinned. "You're teasing me now, Lily Woods. Your grandmother says you're peas in a pod, you and that wild grandfather of yours, even with your hair as sun gold as his is jet."

"Does she?"

"Aye."

"Well, I suppose she ought to know."

"She knows a great many things, like soaking the oats to make the smoothest porridge I've had my tongue glide over since—" He stopped himself suddenly. "For a long time."

"She's using your cousin Mrs. Delaney's instructions. Gran writes out a great many things. To find out what she's thinking, she says. But now she's out walking—to bargain with Mr. Tinkor the beekeeper so you can have honey with your cream and not have to suffer our maple syrup."

"She's not!"

He looked amazed and delighted, and I liked the look of these things on his face very well. "Do you think any of us were so spoiled?"

I continued. "But for you, listen to her words—'the boy's so far from home, and Mr. Tinkor's just down the hill.' "

"Now I know you're teasing me."

"Hugh, we're happy for your company. Is that so hard to understand?"

"It is, aye."

"Why?"

His face clouded. "Maybe because I'm an ignorant, bog-trotting Irishman."

I frowned. "And maybe you didn't read the letter very carefully. The one you carried across the water to us?"

"Letter?"

"The one Uncle Nathan delivered and Gran read us until her eyes burst with tears in remembrance of our Mrs. Delaney. That and your resemblance to Daddy Asher's friend Quinn have given you an honored position, Hugh Delaney, whether you care for any of us or not!"

He was silent a long time and stared at the white sheets and light quilt. "Where's the letter now, Lily?" he finally asked, saying my name in the quietist voice I'd yet heard from him.

I smiled. He'd made my name sound musical. "In the hearth room. Would you like it returned?"

"I would indeed. If you please."

5

THOMAS COLE'S LEGACY

D id you not hear her, Lily Woods? Did none less than the *pi-shogue* herself say I might be up and walking now?"

"The *pish*—?"

"*Pishogue.* Is she not the wise woman of this place? Your great-grandmother Constance?"

I smiled. It was the first time Hugh had slipped into his first language without apologizing, and it pleased me. He was also talking in questions, and so was feeling better, to my way of thinking.

That day Gran Constance advised me to take him on a stroll of the place while she headed a berry-picking expedition. He was doing well, with even the darkness under his eyes turning sallow. Better still, he hadn't seemed overwhelmed by the barrage of family and friends who'd come to take a look at the kin of Quinn Delaney.

My relatives had not visited all at once, of course. He'd met Aunt Susannah, my father's twin and the daughter who looks most like Daddy Asher, the first day. With her was the farm family that included her husband, Gilbert Jenkins, and firstborn Michael, a gifted husband-man like his father who'd planted his field in April and his young wife, Betsy, some months earlier. Both field and family were due for harvest in the fall.

Martin and Charlotte were the younger Jenkins children, born on either side of my fifteen years, who were more like brother and sister than cousins. It was important to me that Hugh like them. He took to their plain and forthright ways straight off.

Hugh'd also met our family's oldest member, Gran Constance's second husband, Mr. Steenwyck, the father of my Boston uncle Ross and New York City uncle Charlie. Mr. Steenwyck is nearing ninety years now, and was once my grandparents' schoolmaster. He sat straight and tall in the chair set out for him beside Hugh's bed and proclaimed, "This boy looks in need of some Homer!"

Mr. Steenwyck then proceeded to read to him of Greek heroes until sent home to Gran Constance for supper. Hugh didn't look any the worse for the ordeal, for Mr. Steenwyck still has a fine declaiming voice, though he sometimes forgets what house he's in or the day of the week. He remembers what prompts young boys to read further on their own, too. He left the book with its mark in the midst of the battle for Troy.

With Uncle Nathan still downriver with Mama, Aunt Pen came for tea with Albert and Eliza, active children who bounced on Hugh's bed without a reprimand or complaint. It made me think Hugh was used to having children about—that and the way he joined in the string game they wove between his fingers. I wondered again about his family. Were there little ones? How could they all be gone, I had made bold enough to ask Father McKiernan, the chaplin of Saint Joseph's chapel, when I met him at a crossroads.

"Most written reports of the famine are from British sources, Miss Woods," he had informed me gently. "The sources we American Irish count more on are the ones from the mouths of the teeming masses coming up from the port of New York. Those tell terrible tales of whole families found dead by the roadsides. With nothing left to eat, not even diseased pratties—potatoes—their mouths are green from trying to fill their bellies with grass."

The thought of Hugh's painful thinness, of his family in such a state, had left me with a gnawing at my own insides. "How are such things possible?"

"Indeed how, in a country that exports food while her people perish?" The priest had passed his hand before his eyes. "Ah, forgive me. I have heard too many of their stories. Such as you should not be scolded but thanked for your generosity in helping the survivors find a new life here. It will not be wasted. Ireland's greatest export to the United States will be its people. This I promise you."

"What is it troubles you, Lily?" Hugh asked, pulling me and my thoughts back to the airy room still scented faintly with Saint-John's-wort. "Do you think I'll be falling off your great mighty mountain again if you do as you're bid and come walking with me?"

I smiled and yanked the shawl from his bony knees. "Not if I don't push you off," I told him, offering my hand.

Outside, Hugh breathed deeply of the mountain air. In the distance we could hear a flock of my young cousins giggling as they accompanied their mothers and our two grandmothers to where the wild strawberries grew. There was longing in Hugh's eyes, I thought, to follow them.

"Have you been to the tops of all these peaks, Lily?" Hugh asked as we reached the pine grove clearing.

"Oh, yes, starting with Round Top when I was still in Mama's arms or perched on Daddy's shoulders. Later Daddy Asher conducts the Grand Tour. It tickles him to call it that, after the fancy travels the wealthy Europeans talk about. Our Grand Tour comes to every one of us to celebrate our twelfth birthday. It's a circuit climb of the entire ring in his company." I swept my hand over the mountains that protect our high valley.

"How long does it take, this tour?" he asked.

"About a week."

There it was again. A deep longing in his face.

"I can show you what it looks like from the peaks," I offered.

"How?"

"Come," I said, leading him toward the Sutherland house.

"You're a mystery, Lily Woods," Hugh said.

The words thrilled me. Was I not merely Joshua and Sarah Woods's awkward second daughter, failed even at staying away from home long enough to achieve a finishing school education? Was I a mystery? Aunt Pen says it was her mystery that drew Uncle Nathan to her and Uncle Charlie to her sister, down in New York City. Others called it a Gypsy curse. A woman should cultivate her mystery, she further advises, so that her man remains interested in her. *I must ask her how to do that,* I decided as my hand grew warm holding Hugh Delaney's.

I was careful to enter the big house from the front door, thinking that taking Hugh in the back way might provoke him to start calling me Miss Woods again.

None of us are ostentatious. Still, the grand proportions of the Sutherland place must have dismayed my guest. Our stone house had been a wonder when built back in 1701, but was almost in ruins when Gran inherited it from Squire Sutherland. She and her wilderness husband breathed new life into its grand rooms, and birthed their children in the cozy borning room beside the hearth kitchen. But Daddy Asher always preferred the outside and his horses, so Gran and my father were the chief architects responsible for making the Sutherland place the Woods family's seat. When Gran and Daddy Asher struck up the mountain to build their cabin, she left the place in Daddy's care. Early in his marriage Daddy constructed a north tower, then a rear wing of rooms for Mrs. Delaney.

I brought Hugh into the main hall and up the spiral chestnut stairs to the third-floor gallery—bounding up too quickly, I realized, when I left him panting in the doorway. I pulled the heavy drapes Gran had hung to keep the room in complete darkness when her treasures were not on display. Hugh's eyes widened with amazement as he took in the paintings that covered the walls from ceiling to floor.

"What is this place?" he whispered.

"Gran's art gallery. These before you are all Mr. Cole's—paintings of the peaks around us, see? My family had a deep and abiding friendship with Thomas Cole. My father and grandfather met him after one of his first excursions to our mountains. He taught Daddy Asher how to play the flute."

I led him down the room's length. "Some say it's Gran's only indulgence in the frivolous—her becoming a patron of Mr. Cole and his students, then asking them to choose more works of art for her on their European excursions. But I look through the gallery, or hear my grandfather's flute, and believe them as necessary as air to breathe. What do you think, Hugh?"

I just then realized that he was no longer beside me as I walked toward the section that included efforts from Uncle Reuben and Aunt Tascha, two of our generous friend's students. He stood before a massive painting of the view from the heights of Stony Clove itself. I returned to him. He took no notice of me until I touched his arm.

"I'm there," he whispered. "I'm in the picture."

"Mr. Cole was most gifted that way, yes," I assured him. "We all miss him. He died about two years ago now."

"Lily," he called again in the barest whisper, "I'm in the picture."

"No, you're not, Hugh. You're with me, in my grandmother's gallery."

I took hold of his arm, trying to assure him he still had substance. He blinked a few times, as if coming out of a dream. Then he scowled. "You must think me a fool."

I smiled. "Not without thinking myself one! Now you see how I've been well trained in losing myself in the clouds."

"Is that all it is? This isn't a place of spells?"

It was my turn to scowl. "Of course not! They're paintings, wonderful paintings, nothing more! You've heard things about us in the town—you've listened to nonsense, of envious people trying to bring us down again!"

"I haven't done any such!" he protested as I yanked the drapery closed and put the room in darkness again before joining him at the door.

"You will. Some are as ignorant as you yourself and think Mr. North some agent of the devil, there at his forge."

"I . . . am not yet used to the sight of black people in this new world," he protested. "And my people have tales of the devil being black."

"Or red, like the savage you thought Daddy Asher was upon that first sight you had of him?"

"I think your grandfather has long since forgiven that transgression, Lily Woods, if only because of my resemblance to my kinsman, his friend. Will you?"

I looked away. "You made no insult to me, Hugh Delaney," I maintained.

"Did I not? Where I come from, an insult to one family member is an insult to all."

"I mean only this: that you must decide for yourself what we are here, beyond the clove." I closed the gallery door behind us.

"Might I come back sometime?" he asked quietly.

"Three days a week my grandmother opens her collection for two hours in the afternoon. Any may come then."

"So it was your hospitable duty to a member of the public I was treated to just then, along with your lashing tongue?" he asked, watching my face. It reddened with shame at my own behavior.

"Now you have evidence of why no school could finish me," I admitted ruefully.

"Finished? No. There's too much fight in you to ever be finished, Lily Woods."

He'd misunderstood my meaning of "finishing," connecting it with pugilism, but what he'd said so charmed me that I didn't correct him.

His tired eyes. My manners. I'd brought him into my home without offering him anything to eat or drink. "Shall I put a kettle on?"

"Have you honey?" he teased.

"I'm sure I could come up with a spoonful, after my poor, limping gran trekked all the way to Mr. Tinkor the fiddling beekeeper's for a supply."

"Then I wouldn't refuse a cup of tea," he said, smiling.

I led him downstairs, then through the library, where my father and Gran catalogued the squire's collection and added their own favorites for as long as I can remember.

Hugh scanned the titles and the seat that curved below the room's leaded glass pane window box. That perch was, as always, in artful disarray from Mama's habit of reading three or four volumes there on warm afternoons. I missed my mother then, looking at this reminder of one of her pleasures. I wondered if her relatives downriver were being kind to her and Jane, and when they were coming home, where I was sure Jane would become well again.

"Is this where Mr. Steenwyck found the story of the Grecian queen and the great war fought over stealing her?" he asked quietly.

"No. That copy of the *Iliad*'s from his own collection. Mr. Steenwyck was a schoolmaster before he married Gran. Then he held all manner of professions before becoming a town justice, which is what my father is now. Mr. Steenwyck never lost his love of the story of the fall of Troy. He treasures that book, Hugh."

"I will not harm it any!"

"I didn't say you would. Only that he honors you with the trust."

He frowned. "What kind of honor is it that leaves me wondering what will be happening next in the story? If that Achilles fellow is going to sit pining after his friend or get back into the fray like a man?"

I stifled a giggle behind my hand. "I think he hopes you'll read on yourself, and thus keep your healing time pleasantly passed."

He growled at me, at the shelves of books in the room. He walked to

Mama's reading spot and stared out the diamond-paned windows, losing himself in the view of the horses prancing beyond the beveled glass. He was hungry, I reminded myself, and I was chatting like a magpie instead of feeding him. I bade him follow me.

The kitchen hearth had been unchanged almost since the squire's time. All the women in my family had learned to cook on the open hearth, except for Aunt Pen and the Steenwyck city women who'd closed up big hearths like ours long ago and used more modern cookstoves.

I lit a small fire in the hearth, where Hugh's cousin Mrs. Delaney had toiled for so many years, as her kinsman inspected the chinking and marveled at the Dutch oven.

"What's this?" he asked as he lifted a latch and opened the door built into the stone beside it.

"A closet."

"For what? It's empty."

I joined him at the side of the hearth. "Is it? We used to store the broom there. I wonder what Mama's done with—"

"It's a priest hole, Lily!" he proclaimed.

"A what?"

"We have them in old houses in Ireland as well. From the Penal Law days, when the laws did not allow the legal existence of any such person as an Irish Catholic. These were times of oppression, when the priests were hunted up and killed. The ones who sympathized, they'd hide the priests away in places like this when the authorities came."

"But this is America, Hugh. No one hunts priests here."

"But you did maybe? In times past?"

"I don't think so."

"Who do you hunt?" he asked, unconvinced, as he stepped inside. "There's a fresh scent of fear in this space."

That was Hugh Delaney's first inkling of the secret family business. And my first thought that he might betray us.

"Get yourself out of there! Stop saying such things!" I yelled, a chill running down my arms.

He stepped out of the darkness and latched the door. "I'm sorry, Lily," he whispered. "I meant no offense to you, or this house, or your country. Such things are common where I come from."

"Not here!" I insisted.

"Aye. Of course. Surely."

"What are you bowing for?" I demanded, when, truth to tell, he was only nodding his head.

His lips compressed. "Habit," he admitted, "groveling. When someone with wealth and power raises the voice, you see?"

"Oh," I barely whispered, turning to the fire. "Tea's on," was all I trusted myself to say. Then, "Please sit."

The tea and pound cake brought the flush of color back into his cheeks. The short walk had exhausted him, though I expected he'd not admit to it if his hand were held to the fire.

The set of bay windows that my father had had built into the kitchen's stone wall to please Mrs. Delaney allowed Hugh's gaze to wander again toward the antics of two mares and a lively gelding out back.

"What breed are your grandfather's horses, Lily?" he asked shyly.

"They don't have a name. They all have the blood of the spotted horse Daddy Asher brought back from the western wilderness a long time ago. That one mixed wonderfully well with the horses Mr. Morgan was breeding over in Vermont for speed and strength. Ours are gentle-tempered. And strong for farm work. But most can gallop like chargers when given their head." I bit my lip. "Do I speak too much on them, Hugh?" I asked.

"You cannot talk too much about horses."

"You do ride, then!"

"I did. Town to town. On borrowed horses of our landlord's stables, as the Irish are not allowed to own a horse worth more than five pounds. But I rode, taught by my father. Years ago, now."

"I don't believe it's something you forget."

"No?"

"No," I assured him. "My father was away for years in Boston getting educated, but whenever he came home, the horses knew him, and he could gentle the young ones, like Daddy Asher taught all of us to do."

"It's a gift then, maybe."

"It's a gift, surely."

He grinned suddenly at the cadence that had crept into my talk. "Your Celtic ancestors must have traveled across the sea to Scotland in recent times, Lily, for you've the temper and the fond speech of an Irishwoman, both."

"Maybe my ways come from closer to this new country. Maybe it's a gift of another Delaney. The one who helped raise me."

He looked around his cousin's domain. "Your servant, aye."

"She wasn't our servant," I insisted hotly. "Mrs. Delaney was our dear friend."

"We don't regard being in service as a demeaning place, Lily," Hugh said softly. "So long as we are still human in the eyes of our masters."

"Do you think of colored people as human, Hugh?" I ventured carefully.

He winced. "I must think on this question, here in America?"

"Yes. Here among us, especially."

"Because America holds black people as slaves in your south land?"

"Yes."

"Why is this permitted?"

"Because they are needed. To work the land."

"As were we, before *an gorta mór.*"

"An—?"

"The famine. Before it we worked the land, paid our rents and tithes to the English Church. Now the landlords would just as soon we all die or emigrate, so they can raise their cattle for market. Marcella's young man deliberately got himself caught stealing so he could be transported to Australia. 'I may be in chains,' said he, 'but at least I will be fed.'"

"That's how the Africans came to America, Hugh. In chains. With little hope of gaining their freedom for generations. Mr. North was born in slavery. To a branch of my mother's family down the river."

"And he does not hate you for it?"

"No. Another branch of my family offered him land of his own, here beyond the clove."

"And what branch might that be?" he teased.

"You know that. Daddy Asher remembers right well not being treated as human, you see. Long ago he was in service to the Chases. They did not see him as human. They beat him something fierce."

"Asher Woods beaten? That great oak of a man?"

I smiled. "Not then. He was a child when in service."

"And when grown he did not kill them all?"

"No. But he rode right into their great hall, with my gran in the saddle with him, and threw down his purchase price, to free us all of the Chases forever. Imagine!"

"Your gliding tongue makes it easy for me to do so, Lily," he said, his eyes fired, his finger stroking a path down my cheek. There was a heightened color in his which I found most appealing. How had I gotten so far afield? I could only think of our sweet Mrs. Delaney as I stared at the comely face of this gift of hers, whose shy touch I wished emboldened. And whom I wanted somehow to taste. I felt my face flame and directed my glance to my lap.

"M-mama and Jane and I," I stammered, "we used to work beside your cousin, not above her, in this kitchen. She looked after us children, it's true. She tried to look after you and yours, too."

"The letter, you mean? Saying I might come here?"

"Yes, and other letters. She sent your mother money as well."

"No. We got no money."

"But Gran used to help her draw bank draughts to send to your family."

"The priest. The one who drank too much poteen. McCarthy. Marcy always said we shouldn't trust that one."

"Priest, Hugh?"

"At our parish. After Mam died. He . . . he said we were too ignorant to understand the letters and—what did you call them?"

"Bank draughts?"

"Aye. He kept them, everything, all but that last letter. Marcy stole it back, cleaved it to her always, along with the name Mam gave to her when dying, of Captain Woods in New York State in America. She made me promise to seek ye out, there on the crossing."

"Your escape from slavery," I whispered.

His hand, already lost in his black curls, fisted. "She was bright-minded, Marcy was. Like you, Lily. It should be her having this fine tea with you now." He stared at the crumbs on his plate.

I touched his sleeve. "Her brother keeps me good company," I assured him. No more lessons on slavery, I told myself, though I could feel the power of Jane's disapproval at my squandering this opportunity to instruct. "Hugh? Perhaps you'll find more answers in your cousin's room," I suggested softly.

He lifted his head. "She had a room? A room of her own?"

"Yes. Two, really, if you count the little parlor next to her bedroom.

Daddy built them onto this hearth room, the same time he made her the set of windows overlooking the back meadow. She was near to seventy by then, and he didn't want her climbing the stairs anymore. Mama and Gran put all Mrs. Delaney's things in a trunk under the bed. I suppose they're yours now, you being her only living kin."

"Mine? Do you think so?"

"Well, there are enough lawyers in this family for me to check the propriety of it, that's for certain sure! But I believe the evidence is in your favor."

"Hello the house!"

The bright cry of our post rider interrupted our deliberations. I jumped up from my place by the fire, rifled through Mama's accounts desk for coins to pay for the receipt of any letters, and was out on the porch before he'd dismounted. By the time Hugh joined me I was waving to the rider as he headed off on a mount Daddy Asher had trained.

I sat in the sun on the back porch steps and, as carefully as my shaking hands would allow, broke the seal on my mother's letter. I lost sense of everything—the warm sun, the June breeze fragrant with the scent of honeysuckle, even of Hugh hovering beside me as I read.

"What is it, Lily?" Hugh finally called me back into the world of my home, my valley, my mountains.

"It was worse than my downriver aunt let on, Hugh," I whispered.

"Worse? For your sister, you mean? In the fire?"

"Yes."

"What does it say, Lily?" he pressed.

I felt my usual ability to speak to overflowing leave me.

"Here. Read," I said quietly, handing him my mother's letter.

He fisted the paper, then threw it to the steps before he took my arms in the grip of hands strengthened by the grandmothers' care of him. "Lily!" he yelled. "What does it say?"

"That my sister burned her hands trying to get to trapped girls and women—her students. They died in the fire."

His changeable eyes went dark with fear.

"How many?" he whispered.

"Thirteen."

He crossed himself, as I've seen other Catholics do. *"Dia Dhuit,"* he breathed. Whether his words were a blessing or a curse, I didn't think to ask.

6

SECOND SISTER MOUNTAIN

Father McKiernan put out his hand in greeting. Hugh only stared at it. I wanted to shake him. Daddy Asher's presence—intrigued, tolerant—kept me from doing so. But this small, energetic man was not Hugh's home priest, stealing the money Mrs. Delaney sent his family. Father McKiernan was a good man, a holy man like my uncle Charlie, who is a pastor down in New York City, working among immigrants. We'd known Father McKiernan for years.

He tried to thaw Hugh's sullen look. "Lily tells me of your recovery and the good company you've been to her while her mother is tending to her sister Jane."

Hugh looked daggers at me then, as if I'd told a family secret. I'd told no secrets. I thought I'd been good company to him in return, while we went through his cousin's possessions. I had a fond memory for every small object—the pictures of angels and saints from her house in Albany, the botanical drawings her son had made of native plants, all the things we children had made for her over her years with us. And her will rested on top, leaving all, including her small savings, to any of the family of her husband's brother, Christy Delaney— Hugh's father. The names of the seven children were listed neatly beside their birth dates. Hugh's was next to Marcella, two years his elder. He'd run his fingers over the names after I read them aloud, then left the house for a solitary walk in the piney woods. It was something I could have seen my grandfather doing to remember his own birth family.

"Do you wish to stay with us?" Daddy Asher asked Hugh now.

"No, sir. I can make my way."

"Father McKiernan comes to welcome you, bring you to Stony Clove. To introduce you to—"

"I'll not need help, thank you just the same, Father," Hugh ground out without looking at him.

I wanted to explain to the priest about that other one, McCarthy, and that Hugh was not always so rude to his elders. But he already had an inkling of the source of the trouble between them, I think. Father McKiernan's gentle smile was in his voice. "I'm only a circuit riding priest, and my means is a cart led by a mount provided to me years ago by your generous host. Did you expect a bishop to squire you into town, maybe?"

"No, Father. Not at all. I'll walk. It's my resources, you see. I have only my cousin's trunk, and were I to spend my inheritance on masses and such for the starved members of my family, many as they are, you see, I would have no start in my life here."

"Oh, son," the priest said sadly, "I'm not after your money. And the ones you lost will rest easy when you find your way in this new country, not when you pay their masses. Hugh, I only wish to provide your transportation to Mrs. Kearney's boardinghouse, before I'm off around the mountain to Conesville. We have a small chapel near the free-labor cotton mill; perhaps Lily's told you of it? I try to come by once a month or so to say mass. I'd be happy to see you there. But I sell nothing. If you don't count the penny candles under the statue of Saint Joseph."

Hugh looked from me to Daddy Asher. Looking for what? My grandfather smiled. "Don't glance my way for a yea or nay on the truth of this," he warned. "I haven't seen the inside of any kind of church in decades."

Father McKiernan chuckled. "Captain Woods sees God in everything, I think, Hugh. He must, to have so much of God's goodness living inside him."

"Now, Father," Daddy Asher chided, "you listened to too much of Mrs. Delaney's balderdash on that subject."

"Blarney, sir, not balderdash! Please, a little respect for your departed friend. She could tell a good story, I'll admit. But I have eyes. And when I see the respect you harbor for women and children and animals, and your pride of place, and your open door to wandering travelers, I think one of your ancestors must have graced the byways of Erin."

Daddy Asher threw back his mane of straight glossy hair to laugh at the notion of being any part Irish.

"You cut me to the quick, Captain Woods," Father McKiernan intoned in mock offense. "Do you not know that our Saint Brendan the Navigator fished North Atlantic waters for souls many centuries before Columbus? I'm sure one or two of his crewmen might have decided to adopt a new county when he saw the beauty of Mohican women!"

I watched Hugh's reaction to their banter. "Are you from Kerry, Father McKiernan?" he asked.

"Indeed, Hugh. I was raised on a farm outside Muckross. It's been nearly twenty years since my mission here in America. Are you still able to hear my county on my tongue?"

"Aye, sir. Father."

"And you knew a good Kerryman once, maybe? Is that why your scowl is gone?"

"A hedgerow teacher," Hugh admitted, "who wrote fetching ballads." I saw fond remembrance in his face.

"Ah, the teacher-poet—that's what Kerrymen are blessed most as! I hope God and Saint Brigid keep your teacher well, Hugh Delaney, for I think he's paved the way for you to accept my company this day!"

Father McKiernan was right. Once he had proven himself from that same Irish place as Hugh's teacher, Hugh joined him on his journey into the town of Stony Clove and took the job offered at the mill and his room at Mrs. Kearney's. I wondered at it, though I shouldn't have. Had I not burst into tears at the sight of a Morgan horse from my boarding school's window once?

I rested under Daddy Asher's protective arm as Father McKiernan's cart traveled toward the cleft path that led away from us.

"Is it too soon to let him go?" I asked.

"It's time."

It was impossible for me to imagine life as Hugh Delaney now faced it in the town of Stony Clove, without family.

"Do you think he'll come to think us strange, sir?"

"That will be up to him, Lily."

"Hugh reminds me of your horses, Daddy Asher," I said.

Many would have laughed at the notion, but not my grandfather. Father McKiernan was wise to see through to the heart of a man folks called Ginny Rockwell's heathen, to his respect for all things with the breath of life.

"How is Hugh Delaney like the horses?" my grandfather asked.

"His fears. They come from such unexpected places. Who would have thought Hugh to be afraid of you or Mr. North, or a Catholic priest? Why would looking at Mr. Cole's painting cause him to go pale? He's like Little Coy or Two Hearts—intelligent and brave and willing to learn while on a path, then suddenly terrified of a blowing leaf or unexpected shadow."

Daddy Asher nodded his understanding, then added a thought of his own. "For all its fears, a horse won't turn on a friend, Lily, not if he's been raised up gently, with care."

I thought of Hugh in Ireland, watching his family die huddled by the roadside. "And Hugh has not been raised that way?"

"He's damaged, I think. We need to be careful, Lily. These are dangerous times. Come. Let's keep our hands busy so we don't dwell on things we cannot change."

I followed my grandfather up the path beyond the cozy cabin nestled among whispering pines. We eased into our clearing work as if I'd never left his side for a strange, white-clapboard school. I worked through the seedling pines and brambles with my small ax; he did the same with larger obstructions. He used a lever to clear jagged rocks, and together we bolstered them to the side of the new trail, thus easing the way up. It was hard work, but not so hard that we couldn't talk while accomplishing it.

"Why are these dangerous times, Daddy Asher?" I asked.

He was silent, not for want of an answer, I thought, but for the correct way to phrase it.

"Because of the laws we talk about at table," he ventured.

I thought of our lively family discussions, especially since our Senator Seward went down to Washington to fight the "Democratic maladministration," as Daddy called the rise of President Fillmore after Zachary Taylor's death in office. The most discussed topic before I left home in the fall had been the passing of the series of laws that composed the Compromise of 1850. It had admitted California as a free state and settled the Texas boundary dispute. What disturbed our family was the establishment of a stricter fugitive slave law.

"Because of the runaway slaves, you mean?" I asked Daddy Asher as we worked. "And the new law that bids them return, even from the free North? That might send bounty hunters kidnapping free folks like Mr. North and his family to sell into slavery?"

"You listen well at table, Lily. The Fugitive Slave Law does more than bid. It requires us to aid in fugitives' capture."

"Us? Help slave catchers and bounty hunters?"

"Any of us your father chooses to deputize."

"You mean my father is required—"

"To uphold the law, as he's sworn. Even Senator Seward's stirring speech about a higher law than the Constitution are only words in Washington. They must be translated into deeds here."

"No wonder Daddy looks so worn of late."

My grandfather smiled sadly as he dug under an embedded bluestone rock. "Josh has the burden of the family's respectability. Your grandmother gave it up long ago."

"When she danced with you at Quinn Delaney's wake."

Daddy Asher looked up from his task. "Mrs. Delaney wove herself a story around that night of Quinn's wake, did she?"

"You still dance with Gran that way, Daddy Asher."

"What way?"

" 'Like you'd lift her beyond the ceiling, beyond the mountains around, and into heaven itself.' That's how Mrs. Delaney used to say it. Just as it is."

"Lord, Lily, between Mrs. Delaney and your grandmother, you've got the stories alive in you!" He chuckled softly.

"That's a good thing, isn't it, Daddy Asher? That gives me purpose?"

He stopped his work and crouched beside me. "It does indeed."

"But is it important? Like raising your horses and curing folks and helping them with the law and in church and in drawing the burial mounds out west and teaching folks and, and, oh, Daddy Asher, did I do wrong by my sister?"

"Wrong, Lily?"

"Why didn't I agree to go and help at Jane's school when she asked me? Maybe I could have put out the fire! I run fast. Maybe I could have gotten help before the girls were killed, before she got burned—"

He took my shaking shoulders between his large, gentle hands. I felt a deep red slash of pain in his voice. "Don't turn your thoughts so, Lily. It serves no purpose, believe me. Jane and your mother will be home soon. They'll need you strong, not eaten by regret."

I nodded.

"As for your purpose, in the Métis people's way, the storyteller got the place closest to the fire. Do not come to me for sympathy if you do not choose to become a lawyer or teacher or horse trader. Besides, someone must regard the whirlwind of this family's accomplishments long enough to understand why and explain what we have."

I leaned into my grandfather's big, protective hands, grateful for his counsel.

"Jane will be different when she comes home, Lily."

"Different?"

"Changed."

"Damaged, too? Like Hugh?"

"Yes, damaged. Her school—her pride and joy one day, ashes the next, with thirteen under her care gone. She will need us all, Lily. Especially you, I think."

"Why?"

"Because your mother will stand, publicly at least, with her husband, who has sworn himself to uphold the Fugitive Slave law. With her husband means against her daughter's convictions. I grieve for your parents in this burden. My way is more simple, as I never had any respectability to give up, did I, storyteller?" His eyes sobered again. "Ginny and I, we thought Josh best suited to take it on. But how it tears at him and his family, in these trying times. Maybe we were asking too much."

"What do you mean, Daddy Asher? What did you and Gran ask of my father?"

"To guard this place and her holdings for all of you, Lily. Both estate and family grow daily. And nothing pleases me more. But burdens of responsibility come with it. Burdens we've given to your daddy."

"But Gran's brothers help manage her holdings, too, sir," I protested.

"From Albany and New York, yes. Tascha and Reuben are gone west. It's Josh and Nathan and Susannah who chose to settle here in Stony Clove. Susannah married Gilbert Jenkins, who's one of the town's own and is as fiercely protective of her and theirs as I ever was. That will help them find continued acceptance. But Nathan married an outsider, who they whisper about causing spells, as they once did me. And your father . . . well, your father married our enemy."

"No!" I protested.

"I should not talk with you of these things while you're wielding that ax, I think," he said to divest me of my alarm. "I only mean your mother and Jane, being of the Griffin family, provided the link to keep us attached, Lily. To people who have tried for generations to bring us down, to wrest away your grandmother's hold on her inheritance from Squire Sutherland. The Griffins and their hirelings, the Chases, would bring us down, still. Your mother can turn away none of her relatives, no more than any of us could," he explained gently. "The Griffins will use her goodness, her hospitality, to their own advantage, for their purpose."

I felt cold suddenly.

"Some will come home with Jane, I think," he ventured forth. "Then we'll have our hands full."

"But, Daddy Asher, they've never come!"

"Still. I think they are coming now." He shook off the thought like a sudden chill. "We'd best return to our work now, yes?"

I nodded, trying to match his smile.

"Would it be proper of me to ask a fancy schooled lady to plant her derriere on this lever?"

I bounded onto the section he'd indicated. "Only half schooled," I reminded him before we dislodged the rock together.

7

WOODLAND TEACHING

W hen my older students from the colored folks' tiny community
of Freehold were busy bringing in the summer corn harvest, I
still met with Delsey and her brother Hamilton, Mr. North's grandchildren. The Catholic chapel had served as our schoolhouse. Now,
being just the three of us, we met outside it.

As much trouble as I'd had with larger numbers, I had none instructing Ham and Delsey. Neither was yet five years old, and their
efforts at making the letters on their slate boards, at spelling and reading and figuring sums, were a wonder to me. As, I confess, was their
attention to the stories I told under the white birch's shade.

I was telling them one of my grandfather's stories—"The Time Turtle Went South for the Winter"—when I heard the rustling in the
bushes beyond. Delsey's face pinched with fear. She reached for her
reader and tucked it inside her pinafore, then pulled her smaller
brother into her lap. Ham protested.

"Now, you'll never find out why all turtles' shells are cracked if you
don't mind—" I began to scold. Three boys stalked into view.

"These little pickaninnies out to trouble you, Teacher?" Sloat Hill
demanded.

"Why, I believe I have enough rope to string such little coons up for
sassin'," Grat Chase offered, stretching a length of hemp between his
hands.

The children quickly scrambled within my full skirts as I stood. I
rested my hand on Delsey's shaking shoulder as Parslow Chase, Grat's

eighteen-year-old brother and the boys' leader, took a step toward us. "But what shall we do to keep a nigger-loving schoolmistress who don't know her own place well enough?"

"Wait up, Parslow," Sloat Hill protested weakly. "I don't mind funnin' with nigger babies, but a Woods gal's got powerful—"

There. A weakness in Parslow and Grat Chase's ranks. I anchored my stare on Parslow. He must have seemed a giant to the little ones in my care. "You have no business here," I told him.

"And your business here is downright illegal. My granddaddy says so. Town Council ain't voted yea or nay on you schoolin' niggers. We might get mad about you not asking town permission. We might have to burn this here forest school of yours, like they burned out your sister and fried her niggers downriver."

The little ones buried their heads deep in my skirts. That was enough to stoke my anger into full flame.

"And aren't you the brave ones, the three of you! Bothering me and two children who barely reach your knee and never did you any harm!"

"Nits grow into lice," Parslow informed me evenly. He was a Chase through and through. And my family had not had any use for Chases in three generations. I turned to where there might yet be hope.

"Wouldn't your sister be proud of you in this business, Sloat Hill? And is this afternoon's diversion one your ma will be writing up in her *Journal* column?"

Both Grat and Sloat looked at some scattered pine needles that dusted the ground under their boots. Sloat even backed away a step. But their reaction seemed only to further embolden Parslow.

"Me and Grat, we ain't got womenfolk for you to shame us with, Lily Woods." That was true enough. Chase women were known for running off, dying, or otherwise leaving the households. The current generation of bachelors was leaving the county to court women not as familiar with their bad reputations as husbands. They had a strange pride in bringing women low. I saw it in Parslow's eyes as he continued to taunt me. "Now, the folks around my granddaddy's tavern are always mighty interested in what goes on back beyond the clove, what with your screaming ghosts and Gypsies and Indians. All manner of comings and goings. Not all of them haunted, either, like you'd like us simple folks to believe." He took a step closer.

Something flew down between us then. I could make no sense of it at first, something with such length and substance flying to my aid like an avenging angel. "Not one more step!" No, it was not an angel or a young aspen uprooted but Hugh, jumping down from the limb of the white birch.

His very appearance seemed enough to set the first two running. Parslow Chase himself stayed only long enough to say, "If I had my gun—" before he turned, following after Grat and Sloat.

I couldn't imagine what had made three strapping boys flee, with the odds for a fight so clearly in their favor, until I touched Hugh Delaney's shoulder. When he turned I saw the glint of steel in his hand.

"Put it down," I said quietly before kneeling to soothe the crying children still gripping my skirts.

"Was I supposed to face them with my fists alone?" he demanded.

When he said it that way, I became less shocked by his weapon. "You didn't have to face them at all. Thank you. But you still bear a look that's quite . . . fierce, Hugh, and it's frightening the children. Please put your knife away."

He glanced down at his hand. "Oh. Oh, aye."

I struggled on without success to calm Ham and Delsey. Sad to say, they'd been tormented by plenty of youths with Hugh's accent.

Hugh yanked out a handkerchief from his back pocket and squatted beside Ham. "Here, give us a blow, then, lad," he said over the child's blustery sobs. To my surprise, Ham obeyed. When Delsey wiped her nose on her sleeve, Hugh frowned, producing a second frayed handkerchief from the same pocket. He made it flutter before her teary eyes. "Sleeve for the arm, rag for the nose," he intoned, very much as Mrs. Delaney used to do with me. "Unless, of course, the rag's . . ." He shoved it deep into his fisted hand, which he then opened, revealing nothing. "Disappeared."

"Where'd it go?" Ham demanded.

Hugh grinned. "Now, I don't claim any earthly control over what's magic, but let's try . . . in Lily's ear!" he finished, making the cloth appear from exactly there! All three of us giggled out our excitement.

"Why, Hugh, that's wondrous!" I exclaimed.

He snorted. "Country folk are easily amused."

"And what so amused you that you sat in that tree spying on us at our lessons?"

"I . . . was there when you came along," he stammered. "Just . . . you know, climbing."

"And didn't think to come down and introduce yourself the whole time?"

He looked a tad wounded now. "Why, Lily, you already know me."

"I do indeed. Hamilton and Delsey North, this is Hugh, kin of my friend Mrs. Delaney. Hugh Delaney, may I present . . . no, wait a minute, I think I did that backwards," I murmured, trying to remember the proper introduction etiquette between elders and youngers from Mrs. Beech's school.

Hugh touched his cap at the children. "Pleased."

Delsey backed into my skirts again. But to our astonishment, Ham, who moments before had been crying the loudest, opened his small hands to Hugh, entreating, "Up?"

Hugh obliged, then looked my way.

"I'd best get them home to Mr. North's place," I said. "That's the meanest Parslow and his band have ever acted."

"They've been by before?"

"Who do you think was responsible for the rip in my stockings the day you arrived in Stony Clove, Hugh Delaney?"

His face flushed. "Wish I'd sliced them to bits," he growled, which shouldn't have thrilled me in its fierce protectiveness but did.

"You put my baby down, Irishman!"

Kikoyo North appeared, raising a tree branch between her hands. The children's mother was tall enough to carry her pregnancy under her striped shirtdress and apron with a graceful ease, but Hugh stood a head higher. Still, he had no thought of that or his weapon as he lowered Ham to the ground and said, "Yes, mum."

Ham took hold of Hugh's trouser leg. "Don't hurt Lily's friend, Mama," he charged.

Kikoyo looked to me. "This ain't one of them no-use shantytown boys, Miss Lily?" she asked.

"Hugh's Mrs. Delaney's kin, the one Mr. North saw to at Batavia Kill. He doesn't mean us any harm, Kikoyo. He's just now been of great assistance."

"He's out to slice the Chases to bits, Mama!" Delsey announced.

The children's mother put down her own weapon and wiped the side of her lean, careworn face with the back of her hand. "Well," she

said, smiling, "that'd be a service." She approached, walking around
Hugh slowly. "You come to take your kinswoman's place up at Justice
Woods's house, Irishman?"

"No, mum. I've a job at the textile mill."

She cocked her head. "What's 'mum' mean, Miss Lily?" she asked
me without taking her eyes from Hugh.

"It's like 'missus,' Kikoyo. No insult."

"All right," she grunted. "Can't cook, then, kin of Mrs. Delaney?"

He smiled. "I'm better at eating."

"He can make rags disappear, Mama!" Ham proclaimed.

"Can he? You'd best leave the gentleman's leg to himself, son, as
you ain't much bigger than a rag yourself."

Hugh touched his cap brim. "Your children are wondrous fine
scholars, missus."

She squinted her eyes, but kept her stare steady. "When they're
treated decent, like the Woods folk treat them. Like your auntie did.
You still think their granddaddy's the devil, Irishman?"

Hugh's face flushed with embarrassment. "No, Mrs. North. And I
beg pardon for saying such a thing."

"Come get yourself my father-in-law's pardon at the forge, Mr. Delaney," she invited as she made him a small curtsy, just like the kind I'd
not learned properly at Mrs. Beech's school. "I believe it would please
him no end to see you lookin' well, sir." She turned to me. "Is it well
and healthy for Irishmen to look like God forgot to dip his brush at all
when it was their turn at creation, Miss Lily?"

"I believe so, Kikoyo."

"Miss Lily, that parsimonious daddy of yours need some help with
the house and meals while your mama's away?" she asked me then.

"My aunt Susannah's been coming by to help, thank you."

Kikoyo shook her head. "Ain't right, you know, for a man as well off
as Justice Joshua Woods to take advantage of his sister's good nature.
Mrs. Jenkins been looking a little poorly to me lately, too, what with
the work of harvest, and her own family, and helping to sew for the
new grandchild on the way."

"Kikoyo—"

"Now I just say it because she's a good lady, like you all, not except-
ing your proper daddy. I know what overworked be, Miss Lily. Three

deliveries of wash before I can see my babies open their eyes in the morning. But I'll bake a nice buckle for when you bring your young man to the forge, Miss Lily. You like wild strawberry buckle, Mr. Delaney?"

"I'm just Hugh, mum . . . missus. If it pleases you, of course. And I'm sure I'll like it fine."

It won't work, you know," I told him as we watched Kikoyo put her basket of laundry to her hip and trudge up the road.

"What won't?"

"Getting her to call you by your Christian name only. She'll never do that. Best you can hope for is a mister in front of it, someday, when she trusts you enough. She doesn't trust any of us completely. None of the black folk do, I suspect. But then, why should they, with the torments inflicted by the likes of—"

"Shanty boys?"

"Some," I said without looking at him.

"She seems plenty able to take care of them all, Lily," he said, smiling. "After wielding a mighty oak branch? And calling me 'Irishman' like the longshoremen on the docks of New York did, all unfriendly like, when I come looking for work? She must be a terrible scold of a wife, that one."

"She's not a wife anymore. Not since her man got crushed by falling timber while clearing brush for the lumbermen three months ago."

His face sobered. "I'm right sorry to hear that. Sad."

"She was a different Kikoyo just now," I admitted, "when she thought her children were being threatened. She's strong-minded and proud all right, but usually more wary, even meek, around strangers."

"That one? Meek? What's her name mean? Lioness?"

"You'll have to ask her. When you're eating her buckle."

"And how in the name of Cuchulainn himself am I to devour a hunk of metal dressed in strawberries for this woman?"

I collapsed against his shoulder in my laughter. He touched my back and whispered at my ear, "It's wondrous good to see you again, Lily Woods, no matter the circumstances."

I felt a warm rush of pleasure at my cheeks. "My horses are down in the meadow. Can you manage Hamilton, Hugh?"

He frowned at me in a way I was beginning to find endearing. "And what use would I be to anyone if I couldn't haul the pennyweight that this nig—that this little lad is?"

I rolled my eyes, now used to his endless questions that didn't require answers and pleased that he'd stopped himself from saying "nigger." He lifted Ham to his shoulder. "And we're to bring them—?"

"To Mr. North."

"Beyond the clove?"

"That's right."

Did he wince? "Why, Hugh, you don't put stock in the town's stories of spirits and screaming beyond the clove, do you?"

"Not when I've got the estate usurper's granddaughter to hold hostage," he said with a wicked gleam in his changeling green eyes.

I stopped in my tracks. "I'll take you on, with or without your fine knife, for slandering Ginny Rockwell so!"

He grinned. "Do I appear senseless of that, lass? Why else do I hold a defenseless *bab* to shield me as I bait you?"

I shook my head and walked on, knowing he'd follow. How Hugh Delaney could fire my indignation both confused and delighted me. His eyes gleamed bright when he saw Cranberry and Maple picketed in the meadow. The circle of grass around them was cropped short. Hugh eased Ham to the ground, where the boy ran after his sister to pick great clumps of clover for the horses. I braved a look at Hugh then, while he was busy admiring the red and light-chestnut mares. He wore a new cotton shirt under his vest, and his cap was patched neatly in places. He was better filled out and, though still lean, did not look close to starvation. His no longer gaunt face bloomed ruddy, not from fever but a returning health. I was pleased, even if our care was no longer responsible for it.

As I approached the pickets, Hugh leaned over to gently tuck the shirt into Ham's rope suspenders.

"You have the time to accompany us, Hugh?" I asked quietly, not wanting to pry into his job at the mill but hoping he was getting on all right.

"Aye. With so many bringing in the corn crop or helping neighbors with it, we're down to half days. Corn! Why all this fuss over such food? Did my cousin eat corn?"

"She made the best corn pudding. Maybe it's a different kind of corn than what you have in Ireland, Hugh. Promise to try it—some from Aunt Susannah and Uncle Gilbert's first crop? Fresh picked and boiled? You'll see how sweet and good it is!"

He grinned that flashing, surprising grin. "Only because you asked me, Lily Woods."

I leaned over to release Cranberry from her picket then, so Hugh would not see the warmth I felt again coming into cheeks. My darker skin did not show my feelings through as easily as his, but I still feared becoming less mysterious to him. He followed close behind, then reached up to stroke Cranberry in exactly her favorite spot behind her ears.

"Are you a weaver at the mill, Hugh?" I asked, foolishly jealous of the attention he was giving the horse and seeking to distract it.

"Aye."

"That's skilled labor," I realized as I said it.

Now I had his full attention. But it was less friendly than what he gave Cranberry.

"Aye. My father was skilled at it. He was the weaver of six townships around. Before the blight. When there *were* six townships around." His hands went back to the horse.

"How did you learn?" I asked.

Was his pique at me dissolving? "I worked at his knee. He used to take Marcy and me out from under Mam at weaving time, because we had interest. He'd pass it on to us, he said. In the good days he promised this, you understand. So we went from house to house on our landlord's fine ponies, staying a week or so, doing the family's weaving."

"That's when you found the houses with priest's holes," I said.

"Aye, that's right. They are great play places, priest holes are. Marcy was better at the weaving. She had longer, more nimble fingers than mine. But she said I must come, to help her count threads at first, when I was small, could barely reach the loom. But she could count. She wanted company, and somebody to teach, I'm thinking. She was a teacher, a born teacher, Da said." He looked up. "Like you, Lily."

"I'm sure I don't have your sister's skill, Hugh."

"With the books, I mean," he insisted, admiration shining in his face. "I neither heard nor saw the like of it under that tree. It's not some trick of memory, is it?"

"Trick of memory?"

"The reading, Lily. Those wee small children, reading."

"It's no trick. How they love to learn, how hard they work at it! And Kikoyo is determined for them, of course."

His face was suddenly full of longing. "Is that what the achievement takes, Lily? Trying hard? Having a lioness for a mother and a golden woodland angel for a teacher?"

It was my turn to divert my attention to a horse. "That's how it was for you, wasn't it? With your Kerryman teacher?" I asked.

"I . . . I did not have him for my teacher very long. He was arrested for sedition. Then Marcy and me only went to a national school, but that only lasted a few hours."

"Why?"

"Because the teacher there, he scorned us for being what we are. The recitation that began the day was: 'I thank the goodness and the grace/That on my birth have smiled,/And made me in these Christian days/A happy English child.' We never went back to that place."

Unknowingly I'd dredged up a painful memory. I thought to make his smile return with a change of subject. "And what about your weaving? From where did the learning of that come?"

"From wanting to travel with Marcy and Da. To visit the villages, the houses. To put my hands on all the colors of wool and watch the seamstress's fingers fashion what we'd made into clothes. It was a miracle to me."

"And is it again? Do you like the weaving, your life in town and at the mill, Hugh?"

"I make many mistakes. Some of the women go twice as fast at their looms. It's a wonder they keep me on, I'm thinking. The machines are bigger. And the steam hisses and sparks and everyone thinks I'll understand the numbers, know how to fix it, because I'm a man. But I never saw a steam-run mill before that one, Lily. And outside, the tannery and lumbermen lads make fun of me for working alongside females."

"Has that been so bad that your knife has come out before? In anger?"

He looked at the ground. "Have you heard such things, then?"

"Well, I thought your reputation must have preceded you for those three scoundrels to have run off so fast from our company."

"Threatened only. I have drawn no blood. I swear that to you, Lily."

"You don't have to swear, Hugh. I believe you," I assured his anxious eyes. "I am glad not to be skilled in weapons. I'm not sure I would have your forbearance."

"Forbearance? What is it you're saying now?"

"I have often prayed for the strength of a man when teaching some of the rougher ones who are so much bigger than I am. Ones who have no desire to learn, only to plague and torment me. I should be a tutor only, I told my sister, for those whose desire and delight in books matches my own. My sister Jane admonishes me for this. 'Where is the challenge?' she asks. She herself has braved so much that I . . . I feel like a great disappointment to her and my parents."

I put my hand to my mouth, scarcely believing the words I'd allowed to escape.

"Ach now, Lily . . ." he said in the softest, most musical tone, "how can one with so much learning hold on to such ignorant thinking?" It was that brought the tears to my eyes, that and the soft brush of a leaf to my cheek. When I turned to protest, he kissed me, there in the meadow, in daylight, with the children not ten feet away braiding Cranberry's mane.

It was my first kiss, lips to lips, with a man, the boy-man that Hugh was then. He tasted fine, of the licorice whip he'd been chewing on up there in the birch tree. He smelled of the mill's oak walls and oiled machinery, and his new cotton shirt. And he felt so different from me—hard planes, stubbled with prickly afternoon whiskers. It was a wonder, all his differences, fitting so sweetly into mine.

8

JANE'S RETURN

When I came home the day that Hugh Delaney first kissed me, I wanted my mother's company. The big house appeared empty from the road, as she was still downriver with Jane and the Griffins. I tried not to feel sorry for myself. Perhaps if I went to the library, that place where remnants of her seemed most vibrant, I could find some comfort. I imagined telling her about how brave Hugh Delaney was, and how tender and right his lips felt on mine. I greeted our grazing horses and picked oxeye daisies and tiny yellow bird's-foot that grew along our stone walls. If I placed them at her window seat in the library, perhaps that would signal her and Jane home.

But when I entered the library, someone else was in my mother's square of sunshine—Daddy, his reading spectacles dangling from one hand, a book of sonnets in his lap, and his forehead tilted against the ancient panes of glass. He had the tapestry coverlet Mama had brought to America from Scotland draping his knees. His longing for her was there in his face, even as he slept. My family was full of beautiful love stories, I thought, as I watched his chest rise and fall, his eyelids twitching slightly. Were Hugh Delaney and I beginning our own love story, Daddy? I wanted to ask him.

I approached his still form, and pulled the coverlet up over his neatly buttoned silk waistcoat. But before I could complete my task his hand covered mine.

"Lily," he whispered, "are you well?"

"Yes, Daddy," I answered.

"Where are the children?"

"Children?"

"The ones hiding. Afraid. In your skirts. No. That was a dream, wasn't it?" He smiled, sitting up higher. "Never mind. You're home."

I hid my amazement behind a laugh. "And so are you. So early."

"I canceled proceedings for the rest of the day. I can do that, you know." He puffed out his chest in mock pride. "I'm the justice."

I giggled behind my hand, which made him smile again. He patted the place beside him, and I sat there. "Right before I drifted off," he confided softly, "I was feeling quite brave that I hadn't gone running up to my mother's house for her comfort."

"Comfort, Daddy?"

"Inasmuch as I arrived at a place so deserted by wife and daughters."

"Not even your ghost woman for company?" I teased.

"No. I have no sense of Sally Hamilton," he said quite seriously for a man who genuinely prides himself on his scholarship, his firm grasp on reason. "Perhaps she followed your mother downriver. They are countrywomen, you know."

"I know we women, both living and passed on, have all quite spoiled you."

"That's the truth of it," he agreed without any lawyerly qualifications. Then his face grew contemplative. "Lily. It was the strangest dream. I can't quite rid myself of it. Are you well?"

"Quite well, Daddy."

"Where were you just now?"

"Bringing Ham and Delsey to Mr. North's forge."

"Alone?"

"Hugh came, too."

"Hugh Delaney?"

"Yes. He was released early from work, and came."

"To help you teach?"

"Yes . . . in a manner," I amended.

A skeptical look twitched up his fine brow. "You use the same phrases your mother does when she's evading an inquiry, Lily. In what manner?"

I didn't want to add to my father's burdens here at the close of a trying, wondrous day, but between his dream and his being a crafty lawyer I had no chance against him.

"In the manner of coming to our defense when bothered by some boys," I admitted.

He leaned forward. "What boys?"

I told him. His eyes narrowed, as did those of all the men in my family did at the mention of Chases.

"How bothered?"

"Name calling, mostly."

"And threats?"

"None that they would ever dare make good on." I turned toward the kitchen. "Are you hungry, Daddy? I believe there's some soup on the—"

"Parslow and Grat's father once tormented my sister for wearing Indian beads in her hair to school."

"Sam Younger Chase bothered Aunt Susannah?"

"When we were your age, yes. And you know his grandfather held yours in miserable service to that household. All those boys and men are still on hand to spread every vicious rumor about any of us, from their tavern to the county around. We are savage usurpers of the Sutherland estate to them. We always will be, so we must stay on our guard." He took my arms in his hands. "Do you understand this, Lily?"

"But why is the teaching of children to be despised?"

"Because they're children of another race. Different. Not them, so not human. Not deserving of anything but contempt and the most menial labor, even here in the North. What's happening to this beautiful country, Lily? I'm sure this is how it started downriver at Jane's school, too. The name calling. Before she even put her sign out. Secondary Education for Misses of Color. It doesn't sound like a heinous offense, does it?"

I shook my head, my heart breaking with the misery in my father's eyes. He eased his grip on me.

"Jane's coming home. Soon. Lily, I will die before anyone hurts either of you."

"Don't speak of dying, Daddy," I pleaded.

My father released me. "Forgive me. This is a difficult time. And I feel so helpless."

"I do, too."

"Hugh Delaney lent assistance, you said?"

"Yes, sir. The boys—they left running at the sight of him."

"Indeed?"

"Yes, Daddy," I confirmed, hoping he had not seen the gleaming blade in his dream.

"In town," he probed further, "they say the Delaney boy is wild."

"He's not wild with me."

"How is he with you?"

"Gentle. Polite. But interesting."

"Interesting? I don't know if I like the sound of that."

"Daddy, I'm fifteen. Surely you remember being—"

"I remember. Too well."

"Yes?" I prompted. But he would not even look my way. "You wouldn't want me to have to ask your twin sister the details of being fifteen, do you? Of such things as . . . oh, your first love?" I teased.

He pulled his hand through his hair. "Your mother was my first love. So my sister Susannah will tell you I was a late bloomer in love. In everything. She delighted in it. She delights in it still. She's a trying, impossible woman, like the rest of you. And my obligation to Quinn Delaney and his mother does not include losing you to this stranger while you're still a child!"

It was I who took hold of his shoulder then. "You're not losing me; I'm not ready for any losing! I only said Hugh was interesting."

I heard his panicked breathing deepen. "Yes. That's what you said. All you said. And Susannah may have known it at fifteen, but she didn't actually marry Gilbert until . . ."

"Oh, Daddy. Aunt Susannah and Uncle Gilbert? At fifteen? How splendid. That she knew it then. And theirs is a good match, is it not?"

My heart was suddenly bursting with a new family love story, even as Daddy ground his teeth as if I'd torn it out of him.

His voice softened as he took my hand. "Lily. Listen to me. Your defending Delaney won't be there always. It might be best to stop your teaching a while."

I nodded.

"I'm sorry," he offered.

Isn't this what I'd wanted? To be free of following my sister's foot-steps in my shy, clumsy manner? So why did I feel so utterly defeated?

"How is Hugh getting along?" my father asked now.

I brightened, happy to be drawn away from myself and my failures. "He looks well—filling out and stronger. He's a skilled weaver, Daddy. And he has a new shirt and has patched his hat and doesn't cough at all. And he took to Kikoyo's children, and they to him, especially Ham. Might Hugh and I visit Delsey and Ham at Mr. North's forge, Daddy? Kikoyo's invited him, imagine that. After the taunting she gets from the Irish washerwomen, she lit into him at first! But Hugh won her over, I think. Do you think we might go soon, Daddy? Ham and Delsey so love to learn. Perhaps I could tutor them there at the forge a little."

Daddy looked decidedly discomfited and did not give me the quick permission I'd expected. "No. I don't want you anywhere near Free-hold."

"But why not?" I asked, astonished.

"It's not safe."

"Not safe? But, Daddy, none of the colored people would do me any harm."

"Not them. It's . . . others."

"But you've never allowed the will of others to—"

"These are new times, Lily! Dangerous times!" The anguish in his tone alarmed me, and he saw it. "Forgive me, sweet girl," he whis-pered. "This is none of your doing. There may be a way to keep Ki-koyo's children under your wing. I'll speak to their grandfather on it," he finally conceded.

"Thank you, sir."

"I'm so glad you're home, Lily," he said, then took my hand in his. "You appear so like your mother these days. I should cancel court more often, for too soon she and I *will* lose you to some undeserv-ing—" He sat up higher, his head tilted to the window. He suddenly became a different man from the one he usually was to me—Ginny Rockwell's formal, Harvard Law-educated son, favoring her in looks and gentle temperament both. Now a sense-aware, instinctive man sprang like a cunning wolf from his father's heritage. This man was a sacred dreamer, like Asher Woods, who in his sleep could see Delsey and Ham clinging to me, who could hear an approach not even the birds had yet discerned.

"Lily," he urged, "listen!"

There. In the distance. Wheels. Horses' hooves. A carriage was heading toward the house. My father's happy anticipation made him look very young.

"Sarah, Jane," he whispered. Scrambling over the window seat's pillows on all fours, he peered through the beveled glass panes. "They're home."

But my mother and sister were not the only ones in the carriage. The Widow Webber, accompanied by my silk-clad cousins Wilhemina and Gerald Griffin, emerged from the carriage first. The two women almost exploded through the small doorway, their skirts were that voluminous.

"I'll not live to endure such a journey again!"

"My gown is quite riddled with mud!"

"My hat crushed beyond repair!"

"Welcome, Mrs. Webber," my father said between clenched teeth before bolting beyond them to the shadows still inside the coach's passenger compartment. I didn't blame him a whit except that he left me behind to be circled by my downriver relations.

The ancient widow of the Revolution smiled in a way that reminded me of a dog baring her teeth. Hers were small and so even they looked filed that way. Her voice rose two octaves.

"And could this be little Lily?" she asked.

"Yes, ma'am." I curtsied as best I remembered from Mrs. Beech's school.

"The family beauty, I'd say you are," the widow proclaimed, "with hair kissed by the sun and a complexion of one part cream and one part rose!"

"A dusky red rose," Wilhemina sneered, knowing the hard-of-hearing widow wouldn't take notice of her words, but not counting on her brother beside her.

"Tut, tut, Wilhemina, no manifestations of the green-eyed monster," Gerald, now Lieutenant Griffin, returned from the Mexican War, chided his sister.

Beyond them, I could hear my parents' voices. But not a word from my sister. Was she in the coach at all? I wondered.

"Jane?" I called softly.

Gerald took my arm. "She hasn't spoken since the accident, Lily," he said.

"Not spoken," I repeated, as if saying the words again might make me understand them. Wilhemina and her great-grandmother set off on a new rush of pattering talk, but through it I heard only Gerald's "I'm sorry."

My father backed out of the coach. His so recently flushed, happy face was now ashen. He anchored his stance and waited as Mama eased Jane into his arms. Then he turned.

Except for the white, gauzy bandages around her hands, she was my beloved older sister everywhere but her eyes. Those were haunting in their emptiness.

9

ASHER'S SONG

I woke the next morning to the sound of the flute coming from the mound above our horse ring. It was Daddy Asher playing the instrument Thomas Cole had taught him. He started with a Scottish air, then went on to the first song he'd ever taught me when I was a little girl, a Mohican call. As the song continued, I entered Jane's bedroom. She was standing by her window, watching.

Though she did not turn, I sensed she knew I was there. I touched her back as the last notes sounded.

"Welcome songs," I whispered.

She did not draw me to her side, as she often had after our separations, so I slipped my arm around her slim waist. I only reached her shoulder, as she was a very tall woman, taller than most men. That was a legacy of Alexander McKay, whose miniature graces our parlor hearth. I thought my sister's steely, sure strength came from Mama's first husband, too. But that morning I felt, for the first time, stronger than Jane. It confused me greatly. Jane was the one with boundless energy, who never dreamed, but planned, then did. She achieved whatever she set her mind to, from organizing a permanent widows and orphans society at church, to relentless letter campaigns to Albany and Washington about rights for women and slaves, to her school down the river. She had often sought to enlist me in her efforts, and said such activities would sharpen my mind and steer my life's course. "Idle hands, the devil's workshop," she would chide when catching me cloud-gazing.

Now her bandaged hands were idle. Her whole being seemed still. As still as death.

Beyond the window, Daddy Asher stood on the mound and held his wooden flute up over his head. I could see the Catskill eagle's feather wafting from its leather tie.

Slowly, with infinite care, Jane raised one white-bandaged hand to the pane. When she did, my grandfather let out a whoop that echoed off the stone walls.

"He salutes you, Jane," I whispered.

Her empty eyes filled, suddenly, with suffering. She shook her head. I held her closer. "Yes," I insisted, "your courage."

I heard a commotion in the hallway. "What is this heathen outrage perpetrated upon guests?" the Widow Webber demanded, her cries an awful cacophony with the piercing wails of Wilhemina, who had taken Daddy Asher for some cutthroat savage.

My sister's eyes went empty again. She turned from the window. But Daddy Asher's flute had helped her return, however briefly, however bereft. I clung to that thought, that hope of getting my fiery sister back again.

Outside the door, I heard my father's voice, white hot in anger.

"Heathen? That heathen is master of this estate and a thousand acres around, madame! My father may come and go as he likes, and express himself anywhere on this property as he sees fit."

The widow murmured her apology and quieted Wilhemina's sobs. Cousin Gerald's laughter joined the mix. I couldn't wait to visit up the hill and tell the story of Daddy Asher's dawn flute-playing to Gran. I pictured the relish in her dancing eyes.

Is it any wonder that I preferred being part of Daddy's family? On Mama's side were these guests of ours, ones who watched me for signs of—what? My savage ancestry?

Both my parents were sure their guests' visit would be of brief duration. But by the third day of their stay, the widow had taken to calling the Sutherland place their "mountain refuge from the summer heat and pestilence" that can sometimes inflict the communities in the lowlands downriver.

Imagine! Such words even though they spent little time out of doors, whether in the sunny meadows or by the shady creek! They enjoyed Gran's art gallery space, and the parlor, and the food that

"Only her hands."

"Do they hurt?"

"She doesn't say."

I saw Mr. North rest his hand on his grandson's shoulder. "She say anything yet, Miss Lily?"

"No, sir."

"That's a mighty shame. She's a fine lady, your sister. She had fine things to say, too. About us all being God's children, and all."

"Yes, sir."

Behind us I could hear my downriver relatives' disapproving "tsk" at my addressing their servant-turned-artisan as sir. He seemed to sense it, too, and turned his young charges away from our company.

"Mr. North?" I called him back. "Jane—she likes my grandfather's flute music, I think."

A smile creased the blacksmith's face. "That so? Our Delsey here plays, too—something fine. You got your mouth organ in your pocket, Delsey?"

"Yes, sir," she said, pulling it out. She brushed the well-cared-for instrument on her sleeve, shining it to an even finer luster.

Mr. North raised hope-filled eyes to mine. "You think Miss Jane'd take to a tune?"

"You never can tell." I glanced up to our home's second story. My mother looked hesitant, but both she and my father nodded their permission. "Jane's windows are open, Delsey," I told the little girl. "I'd be obliged if you'd try."

My intentions were good, as my mother kept reminding me afterward.

Delsey began a tune that was deeply mournful but tinged with the hope in her grandfather's eyes. My daddy recognized the spiritual called "Crossing Over Jordan." He'd heard it before, he said, when he was about my age and visiting the widow's house downriver. That's when he first met Mr. North, who helped guide him back to his family on the night the wolf attacked Daddy Asher. At his mention of that time the Widow Webber pursed her lips, which seemed to please Daddy all the more. His Dutch/Yankee looks still favored his mother, but that gleam of mischief in his eyes bespoke him the son of Asher Woods, too, then.

Delsey gained confidence by our attention, and the notes got

Mama and I could never seem to prepare in sufficient proportio
Still, the vast majority of their time with us was spent complaini
Gerald was the only one who proved himself of any use, as he wall
Jane to the creek thrice daily while Mama and I cleared the table af
meals.

Except for meals and the walks with Gerald, Jane was rarely amo
us. We soon realized that in the company of more than two or th
people, my sister became restless and fretful. So she kept mostly
her rooms. Uncle Nathan visited and changed her bandages daily. H
eyes darted everywhere but her hands then. She did not speak, even
him or Gran Constance, who treated her with soothing herb poulti
as well. We should keep talking to her, they both advised, and we d
But nothing we did sparked her eyes alive.

So our hope that being together again with the whole family wou
bring her back into herself seemed to be ill founded. But was it cau
ing greater harm, as the Widow Webber soon proclaimed? We we
her family; how could our presence be adding to her withdrawal?

All but Jane were sitting on the back porch when Mr. North and h
grandchildren came by on a warm afternoon. His original destinatio
was my grandparents' cabin up the hill. But finding them gone ou
Mr. North entrusted me with a note for them once they arrived hom

The little ones delivered some ginger cakes for Jane into Mama
hands, while their grandfather paid polite respects to the widow a
her charges. Mr. North used to belong to the Webber family, back
the time when it was still legal to own slaves, right here in New Y
State. Few folks did, even back then, but the widow of the hero of t
Revolution counted herself among them. The law finally freed M
North in 1829. The widow proposed to keep him on at her estate, l
he chose my father's offer—some of Ginny Rockwell's acreage an
blacksmith's forge. That's when he and his family came north into
valley and changed their name from Webber to North, and be
their part in turning out Daddy Asher's fine horses. The rest of
widow's servants soon followed the Norths and formed the cor
Freehold.

Ham tugged at my skirt, distracting me from observing the p
formality between Mr. North and his former mistress. I stooped s
eyes were level with the little boy's.

"Is Miss Jane all burned up, Lily?" he whispered at my ear.

louder. Soon she was playing the tune with all her heart. Above us, something terrible was happening. The casement windows of my sister's room slammed shut with such force that two of them shattered, the glass raining down on us below. Screams pierced the still summer air, echoing off the stone walls.

"Merciful heaven!" The widow shielded cousin Wilhemina's ears as if she were being assaulted. "What is she doing? Will she jump?" I yanked myself away from both to follow Gerald and my parents, who were racing inside for the stairway.

When I reached Jane's room, I saw a trail of flung-aside debris that led to . . . well, it led to nothing but a wall. My sister was scraping at it with her bandaged hands. When my father and cousin Gerald together finally managed to pull her away, I saw that blood was seeping through the white bandaging. Red streaks ran down her face, too. And she still screamed that unearthly wail. Mama cleared the way for the men to get Jane to her bed. When she saw me, my mother's already burdened eyes took on another measure of misery. She squeezed my hand. "Fetch us a little warm water, will you, Lily?" she asked. "And some cloth?"

I rushed down the back stairs to our open hearth kitchen, where Wilhemina and the widow were consoling themselves by eating the last of Mama's Dundee cake.

"Lily! Have they got your unfortunate sister under control?"

"I need water," I said.

"This is what comes from having no servants! Your mother was well brought up; she should have been able to convince even your father of the necessity—"

"My aunt Susannah and cousins are coming over to help after today's harvest work," I reminded her, quickly going about my task of heating some water over the low banked fire of the hearth.

"True! True! They are a good, sturdy, dependable lot, aren't they? And your aunt's Brown Betty is a delight to the palate. Still, poor relations are no substitute for live-in menials!"

"None of our relations are poor, Mrs. Webber," I informed her coldly as I willed the water to heat. Cloth. Mama needed cloth, too. I turned and fetched white linen from the cupboard. "Where are Mr. North and the children?" I asked, partly because I missed the company of people I preferred and partly to change the subject.

"Oh, Aunt shooed them away in short order," Wilhemina proclaimed. "She has much experience with darkies."

"I've heard," I said, not even guarding the measure of my disgust, but keeping my voice low so only Wilhemina would hear. I was immediately ashamed of behaving exactly as my cousin had on countless occasions.

The widow proclaimed on. "Your poor mother appears weakened by her daily worry, my dear. You have your father's ear. You must broach the subject with him."

"Subject, Aunt? What subject?"

"Come, come, don't say it has not crossed your mind that your sister may never be . . . herself again."

My cheeks flared. I had given that very thought liberty inside my head. My mind had clouded with confusion, and I'd shoved the notion aside, like a nightmare. I'd turned myself toward more practical concerns then, in a way that might have made the old Jane proud of me.

"You must talk with your father about another place for her. Where she'll be safe. Unable to harm others or herself. A quiet place."

I knew what she was alluding to, suddenly. "My uncle Charlie speaks of asylums as horrible places, Aunt!"

Her back straightened with contempt. "Your Steenwyck uncles are radicals, Lily! Dangerous men, working for causes unbefitting of clergymen and lawyers! Working against the laws of this state, this country. I thought your father, in his new appointment, finally out from under their ruinous influence. The Steenwycks must not impress their notions on you. You are our heir!"

I looked from the widow to my cousin, her head bobbing her carefully maintained barley-sugar curls even as her eyes glowed with both envy and disgust. They saw me as their next hope to rid my family of its heritage? To get Gran's assets into Griffin coffers? They'd tried wresting it from Gran herself when she was young, then tried again to get my father to betray his family. Now it was my turn.

I could hardly stumble out of their presence and up the back stairs fast enough.

My mother met me outside Jane's room. "Thank you, darling," she said, taking the cloths and kettle from my hands. Her cheek had suffered a scratch, long and deep, inflicted by her firstborn, trying to escape a building that still burned in her mind.

"Mama, I'm sorry. The tune Delsey played that started this. But I didn't know—"

"Of course you didn't." I couldn't take my eyes from her wound. She touched her face absently. "This is not of any consequence."

"Jane. Is she—?"

Mama smiled. "She's crying."

"That's good?"

"It's better than the silence, those . . . those lost eyes. Lily, she's returning to us, I feel it!"

A forlorn wail cut through the calm, masculine assurances beyond the doorway. I ached for my sister, and in my own helplessness.

"Mama, could I come in, could I see—"

"Not just yet, darling. Your father does not quite share my conviction. He wishes you to ride over to fetch your Gran Constance and Uncle Nathan. Will you do that for us, Lily?"

"Of course, Mama," I said, turning away before she could see my tears. They were sending me away again. Because I was of as little help in my sister's distress as I was in her prime.

10

FALSE COURT

I was surprised to find all the people I was seeking in one place—the parlor of Aunt Pen and Uncle Nathan's town house. My aunt and uncle were acting as impromptu hosts to Daddy Asher, Gran, Mr. Steenwyck, and Gran Constance. They had Reuben's and Tascha's latest drawings of the western Indian mounds spread out atop the piano and were raising glasses of spruce beer to the explorers. Their happy celebration seemed the mirror opposite of the horror I'd left. And would now visit upon them. One more seemed to fit in their midst as if he was born there: Hugh Delaney.

The smiles disappeared at the sight of me, the outsider from the troubled house. Hugh backed himself so far into Aunt Pen's bay-window drapes that she laughed and pulled him out again, her arm linked through his.

I broke up their celebration of my kin's accomplishments with my doleful news. Its recitation scattered them. Uncle Nathan and the grandmothers spun toward Jane at our house; Aunt Pen and the remaining men put their heads together in hurried conference. It was easy for me to slip from their midst and tend my hard-run horse.

I spoke softly as I led her by the reins around the stable yard—nonsense rhymes, plucked from my childhood, a time that now seemed long gone. She nickered back, the blasts from her nostrils easing into regular breaths.

"She cooled down enough for this?"

I turned. Hugh stood beside the pump, a bucket of water in his hand.

"Thank you."

He set down the bucket. " 'Tis the mare Two Hearts, yes?"

"Yes."

He stroked my horse's withers as she drank. "She need a blanket as well, think you?"

"No."

"Aye, then. Your pretty rhymes calmed her along with the walk, I expect."

No question to answer this time. I stood in silence, watching my horse drink, breathing the pine scent from Hugh Delaney's clothes. Within Two Hearts' mane were strong hands, already grown as large as a man's. They could run a loom and lift a child. I longed for their comfort.

"I'm sorry for your trouble, Lily," he whispered gruffly. There was nothing gruff about the way he released Two Hearts and turned to me. One hand touched my cheek while the other drew me under his heart. I wrapped my arms around him, buried myself deeper.

"Everything I do is wrong!" I heard a too-young voice slip out.

Hugh held me, crooning, "Nay, not at all." There was a stillness, a listening about him that put me in mind of the same nature in my father and Daddy Asher. My discovery made me think beyond the rush of excitement that his closeness produced. The thought that I would love Hugh Delaney all my life birthed itself in my heart. It both warmed and frightened me.

I felt his callused workman's thumb scrape the side of my face playfully. "Now that you've cared for your beast, will you look toward this one, who's been lonesome for your company? Would you come walking with me through town in the broad light of day, Lily Woods? Would you take tea? Do you have that much courage in you?"

I giggled at his barrage of questions and turned toward my aunt and uncle's house. "I'll ask—"

"I have done so already. Your relatives, they acted as if I were doing them some great favor. Strange people, you Woods."

My smile disappeared. "You *are* providing them a favor," I attested.

His fine brow arched. "Am I, then? Do you pitch *them* down mountainsides, too?"

I received some stares, walking down the main street of Stony Clove on Hugh Delaney's arm. I didn't mind them, as they were akin to those I remember since sitting atop Daddy Asher's shoulder as a child. The same who fawned over me in my parents' company as my father's place rose in the town's esteem spoke "heathen" and "savage" behind their hands when I was with my grandfather. I had long since learned to maintain my balance among people like that. They will, perhaps, always be among us.

Hugh's long, even strides soon brought us into the Irish section behind Main and Church Streets. He stopped before a freshly whitewashed two-story house set deep among the unpainted shanties.

"This is where I stay, a room up top," Hugh said shyly.

"Are you comfortable, Hugh?"

"Aye, sure. There's my window, see? Close to the stars."

I heard the chinking sound of crockery from inside. There were other boarders having their tea, I realized. My hands went cold suddenly. Walking down the street was one thing, but I didn't like being stared at while I ate. And I was hungry.

Hugh noticed my reluctance, I think, for he hesitated by the doorway, frowning. "We're late for tea. Lateness calls for stealth, maybe," he said, taking my hand and leading me around the house.

As we mounted the back porch steps the door flew open and a little girl burst out, on the run from a woman with a smaller child in her arms.

"Margaret Mary, for shame!" she scolded. "Waking the baby before tea is done!"

The little girl was stopped by my skirts and Hugh's laughter. He continued up the steps and took the fussing baby of about two years from the woman's arms. "We'll look after them out here for you, Mrs. Kearney, if you could spare us a currant scone."

The flustered woman wiped a streak of jam from her apron. "Where is your sense now, Hugh Delaney? You'll introduce me properly to Miss Woods! Then we'll begin our negotiations for late tea." Her eyes drifted to the old willow down the path from the boardinghouse. "A picnic tea."

I soon found myself balancing Margaret Mary and her sister Kate on my knees and reciting "This is the way the gentlemen ride . . ." after their mother and Hugh disappeared within. I was on my fifth or sixth encore of the story game when tea arrived on a tray carried by Hugh, only with his hair combed neat and waistcoat fully buttoned.

"Your ma's got yours in the kitchen," from him was enough to send the children bounding through the door with almost as much energy as they had coming out. I took the worn quilt from Hugh's shoulder.

"Would beneath the willow suit you, Miss Woods?" he asked.

"Now, why am I again Miss—?"

His quick glance at the back window's fluttering curtain soon gave me to know the answer. "Yes, that looks the perfect place," I amended, walking beside him in as stately a fashion as I could manage.

The willow spread a curtain of green around us as we drank our tea and ate Mrs. Kearney's delicious scones. Hugh took big bites when he saw it pleased me. "Refreshed?" he asked as I poured the last of the tea between us.

"Restored," I affirmed.

He stared down at a faded red patch on the quilt, shy suddenly.

"I have something for you, Lily."

"What is it?" I asked, intrigued.

He reached into his vest and brought forth a tissue-paper-wrapped object. I took from a hand trembling a little an object that was not heavy in the least. I cleared away the paper and found a shell hair comb studded with pearls and a gold loop chain. Hugh filled in my astonished silence.

"It's one of a pair. I'll get you the other, too. The shopkeeper's holding it for me. My hours are but half time at the mill, so I took on another job, Lily. The shopkeeper, he says my credit's good, and I might soon—"

"You should not have bought this one, Hugh," I said gently.

"You don't like it?"

"It's the most beautiful thing I've ever seen."

He grinned wide. "Not as beautiful as your hair."

"Hugh—"

"Which I do not say as a form of idle flattery, mind."

"No?"

"Not at all. It is a statement of fact of which you remain unaware, being you ain't—are not—one of them vain girls, always preening. But your aunt Pen says you'll need such things, as you'll soon wind your braids round in fascinating configurations that require security."

"Aunt Pen said that, did she?"

"You don't think I'd be spouting such things on my own, do you?"

I laughed, full and hearty, in a way I hadn't since my sister had come home.

"Lily Woods, you're a slayer of me pride!" my host said, laughing.

I tried again to pull myself from his spell of mirth. "Hugh, you have your own needs you must see to before—"

"Aye. This serves the greatest of them." He laid his hand over mine and glanced behind him at his landlady's back window. "The first of which is to express your worth to me. You have allowed me your company, Lily. Among your family, with children bl—colored and white and Irish. I watch your eyes taking in the words in the books, your balance in the saddle and easy hands on the reins. When I am in your company I find my anchor in this place America. You must know these things, because it will take time to secure myself, to make my place here and make myself half as interesting to you as you will forever be to me. But I mean to court you all that time, if you will allow it."

I felt the comb grow warm in my hand. "Court." Hugh Delaney wished to marry me. "No questions," I finally managed to say.

He arched his brow.

"You're always so full of questions. But you didn't ask this thing of me with any."

"I didn't?"

"No, Hugh."

"Here's one, then. Will you allow me to cherish and court you, Lily Woods?" he breathed out. His coal-black curls had found their way over his forehead again. I was glad, for I had an excuse to reach across the old quilt's weave and the gulf of continents between us. I traced his hairline from brow to ear.

Suddenly, I imagined performing the same tender gesture across the brows of two children. First a girl with black hair, then a flaxen-headed little boy. Who were they? Where had Hugh gone? We were at the village green, I realized, right in the middle of the town of Stony Clove. The little ones glanced up over my shoulder. They began crying, though a military band played a sprightly tune. Behind us. A band.

Soldiers. War. And Hugh. They were our children, Hugh's and mine. Crying for their father, who would join the militia and face battlefields of blood just as Daddy Asher had in the Second War of Independence and his father had in the first. Leaving families to be broken. I must turn. I must see him, tell him. Not to go. The band was so loud, frantically playing "The Girl I Left Behind Me."

I broke the connection between us.

"Lily?"

"Where are you off to?" I demanded.

"Off? Lily, I'm here."

"Why are they crying?"

"It's you crying. Don't. Say no, but don't waste your tears on the likes of me." The bitterness that hovered often about Hugh Delaney had come into his voice.

"You don't understand—"

"Oh, I may be ignorant of a great many things, but I understand this well enough." He turned away, and I saw the heft coming to his shoulders. "I can be doted over as the kin of your nursemaid, can't I?" he challenged. "You'll even grant a kiss or two. But you hesitate to enter an Irish house's front door to break bread."

"That was not the reason for my hesitation!"

"No?"

"I didn't wish to be stared at—"

"Exactly so."

"For who I am, not you."

"I must be too ignorant to see the distinction."

"Hugh, stop this nonsense and hear me!" I demanded.

He looked up over my shoulder toward the approaching hoofbeats. The hard eyes of the Chase brothers delighted in our quarrel as they halted their mounts before us.

"There's a slave hunter party coming through. My father wants you in early to help provide for them," Parslow called down.

"When?" Hugh asked.

"Now, Paddy. If you're quite done with your tea and . . . all else." They rode off, laughing.

"That's the new employment you took?" I demanded, trying to control my rage. "At Garret Chase's tavern?"

His eyes leveled with mine. "Aye," he said. "Mr. Chase. He sought me out, Lily. And I thought, once he offered—"

"Of course he sought you out!" I stood in my agitation. "Do you think there's anything about us they don't know?"

He got to his feet, facing me. "I don't understand."

"They are Chases! The people who owned Daddy Asher."

"That was long ago, now."

"Their whiplashings still show on his back. That family has been plaguing ours for generations. Of course Garret Chase offered more than the mill did, and made the shopkeepers give you credit! That's how they start! Soon you'll find no escape from debts or service. Did they offer you their corn whiskey as well?"

"They say your grandmother owns the mill."

"Do they?"

"Aye. And how was I to prove myself worthy of you on those confusing machines and in her employ?"

"Not by siding with the Chases!"

"Who is siding with any? I push a broom, for the love of God, woman!"

"They pay fair wages at the mill, my grandmother sees to that. Why do those baneful Chases raise those wages for you to push a broom?"

"I—"

"And what did Garret Chase offer you to win the hearts of my uncle Nathan and aunt Pen? And for your false court of my affections, Hugh Delaney?"

He grabbed my arms between his large workman's hands. Not to hurt me, I think, but perhaps to make me aware of their new strength.

"You slander me," he whispered.

Then he released his hold and walked off in the direction of the Chase tavern. He never turned, even when I flung the beautiful comb at his back.

11

RAID

I rode Two Hearts blindly through the clove, glad she knew the way so well. I'd cried so hard my eyes felt crowded by my cheeks. I could not go home like this. Even if my parents and doctoring kin were absorbed with my sister's care, my downriver Griffin relatives would notice my ragged state and give me no peace. I turned my mare toward Echo Lake.

I sought to restore myself, even as the animals approaching its bank were. Tracks of fox, deer, and skunk had preceded mine. Daddy Asher remembers when wolves visited Echo Lake. They took their families to higher elevations, where we still hear their songs in the distance. Our Mohican ancestors came to the lake before they were driven west. They needed a sacred place to cut their hair in mourning for all those lost.

I felt my own loss as I sat beside the still, cold water. Was I so thoroughly deceived by Hugh Delaney? Had all his attentions been calculated? Or was his association with the Chases closer to what he'd hotly protested—the means toward his independence? He was bright-minded. How could he not understand that the Chases' specialty was not to help folks achieve independence, but the opposite, to make them dependent by way of their rye whiskey? They'd spared few tricks in their efforts to catch our family in their web of greed over the years, that was certain.

My mind ached with questions, and the questions brought on the hurt, and the hurt started my tears. I searched through my green serge gown's deep side pockets to find a handkerchief with which I could soak up some cool water and refresh myself. My fingers roamed over pencil stubs and a box of pins until I located the soft muslin. I pulled. A folded scrap of paper came out with the handkerchief.

It was the note I was charged to deliver to Daddy Asher and Gran from Mr. North. I had entirely forgotten it. My own needs could wait. I called Two Hearts with a shrill whistle.

Gran and Daddy Asher were sitting together on the ledge of the blue-stone horse ring. Her walking stick dutifully propped against the wall, Gran's feet dangled like a young girl's as she watched the dance of the horses in the twilight of the day. Daddy Asher sat close, his arm draped over her shoulder in that casual intimacy I loved seeing be-tween them. Their love was a rare thing, the center of all the love matches it had inspired among the following generations of the Woods family. Daddy Asher heard our approach first and swung around, rais-ing his arm in greeting.

"Come, sit with us a while, Lily," he said. I placed the note in his hands, hurriedly explaining the distractions that led to my tardiness in its delivery. Neither asked about my raw and ragged state as Daddy Asher read Mr. North's message.

His mouth set in a determined line, but his eyes blazed with excite-ment as he handed the paper to Gran.

"Shipment," he said. "Tomorrow."

Gran frowned. "Asher. The child," she scolded.

"Lily's not a child. She needs to be told. It's past time."

"If so, it's her father must do the telling."

"Her father's got his hands full contending with that downriver lot."

"Assist Mr. North in what?" I pleaded with them. "Surely the slave catchers cannot take free people, can they, Daddy Asher?"

He turned his head and stared me down. "Slave catchers?"

"Yes. A party of them are at the Chase tavern."

"With the Chases. What matter lives when there's money to be had, whiskey sold and—Lily," he interrupted himself, "you're crying."

"Oh, Gran, Daddy Asher, Hugh has taken work helping out there!"

"Damnation!" my grandfather exploded. "A shipment coming, slave catchers at the Chase tavern, and Hugh Delaney in the mix?"

I looked hard at my grandmother. "It's not a shipment of your paintings coming tomorrow, is it, Gran?"

She winced. "Lily. It must be your father who—"

"The slave catchers," I thought out loud. "Isn't that what was in Mr. North's note, Daddy Asher? Asking for your assistance showing their free papers if the slave catchers come scouting through Freehold?"

"No. That was not in the note, child," my grandfather said quietly. "It was about"—he cast a quick glance at Gran—"another matter."

"Do you sometimes help the runaway slaves get north, Daddy Asher?" I asked. "Is that why we were clearing a new path over the mountain?"

He looked to Gran again. She nodded. "Yes, Lily," he said quietly.

"I think it's wondrous good of you."

He frowned now, though his dark eyes sparked with laughter. "It's wondrous good of Mr. North, who has much more at stake than your grandmother and I do. We're just his assistants." His eyes sobered again. "We must see to these bounty hunters now, if they mean to invade our neighbors' homes in their search. Have you got the free papers handy, Ginny?"

"I have, love," Gran said, her mouth forming that same determined line as her husband's.

"If you'll fetch them, I'll saddle two horses."

After an attempted robbery whose sole purpose seemed to be finding the documents, Mr. North had entrusted my grandparents to keep his community's free papers safe. I remembered a few occasions when they'd brought them forth, along with a promise of legal assistance from Daddy, when several of Freehold's colored folk had been suspected of being maroons—fugitive slaves in hiding.

I touched Gran's sleeve in my desperation. "I know I did wrong in forgetting to deliver the note to you in town! I'm sorry! Do you think they've reached Freehold? Don't send me away. Don't leave me behind again, please!"

Gran touched my face. "You didn't do anything wrong, darling Lily."

"You see?" Daddy Asher chided his wife quietly. "You see what comes of all this damned secrecy?"

"The railroad has thrived on secrecy, Asher."

"Not from Lily! Not from one of our own!"

A long look passed between them. "Walk your mount until we're ready to join you, Lily," he advised softly. "Poor Two Hearts is having a long day."

When we reached the small cluster of cabins beside Batavia Creek, we knew at once something terrible had happened already. Was it because of me? Because Mr. North had trusted me with the note, and I'd forgotten to deliver it? We dismounted in silence. Gran leaned on her walking stick. She clutched the oilcloth-wrapped package containing the colored folks' free papers against her heart.

Wailing sounded from Mr. North's forge.

As we came closer the smell of something awful filled my nostrils. I grabbed Daddy Asher.

"What is it?" I asked, somehow sure he would know.

He did. "Burnt flesh," he answered.

12

RESCUE PLANS

For a fleeting moment I longed to be back at Mrs. Beech's finishing school pricking my fingers with an embroidery needle. But I forced my footsteps to match my grandparents' stride as we entered the small community of Freehold.

We wove our way through silent children held by others only a few years older than themselves. Some backed away, as if we were the enemy, but several touched our hands as we passed, and pointed to the forge. There a few men and women sat patiently having their limbs bandaged or their heads bathed by others. Annie Mitchell, a girl about my age, grabbed Daddy Asher's hand and led us to the side of the forge where Mr. North lay.

His injuries were the most severe. Burns creased his face and both arms, malicious burns inflicted by the red-hot pokers of his own fire. Gran hugged my waist as Daddy Asher waited for a signal of approval from the women tending Mr. North before he squatted beside him.

Mr. North's eyes opened. "Captain Woods?" he whispered.

"Yes, sir."

"Good of you to come."

"What happened here?"

"Slave catchers happened, sir. They got our Kikoyo. Delsey and Ham, too."

My grandfather took in a deep, pained breath. "How?"

"On account of this, sir. Annie?"

She hesitated. "But, Uncle, we ain't safe amongst these no more.

Not since Miss Lily, she cozy with that Irish boy who took up with the Chases."

I felt my cheeks burning. "Hugh sweeps the tavern, that's all," I declared.

"Ain't nobody just sweeps for the Chases," Annie shot back. "He been watching for where Kikoyo and her babies be. From trees. I hear that from Kikoyo her own self."

My voice stumbled in confusion. "He was watching for me, I thought."

Gran squeezed my shoulder. "Of course he was," she said. "This is a misunderstanding, Lily."

Mr. North sat up higher. "The Woods folk be our friends, Annie! Give over that paper to the captain now."

The girl obeyed her elder, but the hardness did not leave her eyes. The folded paper was a post advertisement. As Daddy Asher opened it, Gran and I read over his shoulder.

RUN AWAY FROM SOUTH OF RICHMOND, VIRGINIA, A HIGH YELLOW NEGRO, PHOEBE, NOW ABOUT TWENTY-THREE YEARS OF AGE. FIVE AND ONE HALF FEET HIGH, WELL SET, AND CAN SPEAK PROPERLY. SHE COOKS WELL AND MAY HAVE FOUND WORK AS A HOUSEHOLD SERVANT. VERY SENSIBLE AND ENDEAVORS TO PASS AS A FREE WOMAN. SHE FORMERLY BELONGED TO THE LATE MR. JAMES CUSTIS AND IS NOW THE PROPERTY OF HIS SON, WILLIAM CUSTIS OF FAIR MEADOW PLANTATION ON THE JAMES RIVER. THE REWARD FOR HER SAFE AND UNHARMED RETURN IS ONE THOUSAND DOLLARS.

I thought the paper would rip, Daddy Asher pulled it so taut between his hands. "Kikoyo is not this woman," he said. "We've got her free papers."

"Not Kikoyo's, sir. Captain Woods, it ain't a mistake. Our Kikoyo, she used to be Phoebe Custis. And she ain't free. She came to us. On the line up from Virginia, oh, seven years ago now. Lost her mama on the journey. Found our Henry, though. So we told the white folks, even you-all, that she was a visiting cousin that Henry fell for. She changed her name to honor her African mama's people, our Kikoyo did, then took on North when she married Henry. We thought her safe after a while. But she weren't safe. Neither were the young ones, on account of they come from her."

"And from your son. A free man," Daddy Asher persisted.

"Henry don't count, Captain. Even was he alive now to stand for his family. Delsey and Ham and the one that's soon to come, they from Kikoyo, so they be owned by this man, this Custis, same as their mama is. That's how they figure it in Virginia, sir."

"They'll never reach Virginia," Daddy Asher declared.

Gran and I looked at each other.

Even the blacksmith chided him. "I don't mean to make my family's troubles your own, sir."

"They are our own, Mr. North. While our country allows this horror." He stood, and pressed his hand to our neighbor's shoulder.

In the clearing beside the forge, lanterns appeared through the growing darkness. They were held by a dozen neighbors walking slowly, tentatively, except for Aunt Susannah and her husband, Gilbert Jenkins. But they stepped aside and let Mrs. Jenkins, Gilbert's aunt, speak for all.

"We heard the drivers pass our farms, Mr. North, and knew they were up to no good. We brought remedies and swaddling cloth, and ask your permission to assist you in a neighborly fashion."

The blacksmith looked up past us to the faces of his kin and friends. Not all wanted him to accept the offer. Those faces became unyielding in the fire's light. But there were other expressions, too, which, through astonishment, birthed hope. Mr. North must have decided to rely on their silent counsel. He nodded, even to Mr. Stone, who had dammed Batavia Creek so that North cows had to seek their refreshment at higher elevations.

With permission granted, the near neighbors spread out among the injured Freeholders just as if they were any other families in need. Susannah's long strides reached us quickly. In the shadowy darkness her resemblance to her father and his early American ancestors was striking. She caught her parents and me in one of her robust embraces while her blond farmer husband nodded, grinning behind her.

"Susannah, how did you ever convince—" Daddy Asher began.

"Most of them were Bible reading at the Pike house," she explained. "New Testament, where Jesus whittles the Ten Commandments down to two: love God, love your neighbor. My Gilbert waits until the fellow in the passage says, 'Lord, who is my neighbor?' Well, before the story of the Good Samaritan gets started, he bursts in with the news of the raid on Mr. North's place."

Daddy Asher grinned. "Good timing, son," he said.

Uncle Gilbert's smile widened, and his spectacles reflected both the firelight and his love for my father's twin. "Susannah spoke after me, sir—reminded them of all the times one of the Freeholders has helped us out of ditches, cooked meals for the sick, and gotten our plows mended in time for planting."

Gran slipped her hand into Daddy Asher's. Their pride in their first-born shone from them together.

"What will they think of Kikoyo and her children being taken from here, Susannah?" Daddy Asher asked. "Will their Christian charity extend to—"

Mr. North hobbled over. "Now, Captain Woods, that be a different thing, going against the power of the law. You'll let your good wife and children guide you in this, won't you, sir? Keep you sensible?"

Daddy Asher's smile was like a healing summer breeze in that desolate place. "The law is a slow thing, Mr. North. Ask Josh. But my horses are bred for speed and endurance both. And the trail to your kin is still fresh."

Wait here," my grandfather pleaded as Gran and I brought our mounts up before the Chase tavern. None of us had ever been inside the inn the Chases built with Griffin money many years before.

"We'll do no such thing," Gran insisted.

"Ginny, this is a rough place. Full of unruly men."

"They'll behave themselves better with women present."

We heard laughter behind us. Parslow Chase swaggered out of the shadows, an amber-colored bottle in his hands. "Your great knife-throwing protector out-Chased a Chase, Lily Woods!"

Daddy Asher took a protective hold of my shoulder. "What do you mean?" I asked.

"Just that! He stole my chance to finally break free of this miserable plot of hell! All because those brats clung to him like he could keep them from the block at Natchez or New Orleans! That's where the defiant ones get sent—especially the pretty, high yellow ones, in case you've a mind to track them, Asher Woods! I know. Plenty of slave coffles been through the tavern on their way to the river. If they don't get picked off and scattered by wild Indians," he grumbled in my grandfather's direction. "They have in the past, haven't they? This one was my ticket!" he railed. "They were sent specially, just to fetch the woman and her brats. Easy work. This was the one to get me out, provide my stake. Except the Irishman was of the same mind. They chose him, because he could quiet down that washerwoman and her damned pickaninnies."

"They're gone from here?" Daddy Asher demanded.

"Gone for the river, being we caused a little ruckus in Niggertown, fetching their prizes. You hear? Yep. I expect you already know about that. Five dollars is all I got for beating back those devils. Then they come to the tavern and choose that broom boy to help get them down the river, on a hired steamer—just waiting by the river! Hired a bog-trotting Irishman over me, did I tell you? Just because—"

"Parslow!" A shout came from inside the tavern. "Who are you talking to, you lazy sluggard? Are there customers? Bid them enter!"

The door swung open. Garret Chase stood before us, smiling an affable, innkeeper smile. They said he was a handsome man once, but I only remember him like this—his blotchy face bloated and wasted at the same time, his broad shoulders dominant in their power, his eyes vengeful. A few years older than Daddy Asher, he'd been one of the Chases who'd caused the whitened scars in my grandfather's back.

Garret Chase was my grandfather's opposite. His expression changed as he raised his lantern and saw who we were. "What do you want?" he barked gruffly.

Gran took hold of her husband's arm and spoke quietly. "We've already received the information we came for, thank you." She turned us both toward our horses in that gentle, insistent way of hers. We heard the laughter of both men behind us.

"Did you think a bog-trotting Irishman would side with the niggers, then?" Garret shouted. "They hate them worse than we do, on account of they'll work for lower wages. Don't you overeducated savages know anything?"

Our silence seemed to infuriate them further. "Try to interfere with slave herding now that the new law is passed! Even your almighty justice of the peace son is sworn to arrest you, Asher Woods! Try! We're watching. We're watching your every move."

Daddy Asher's back stiffened, but his long stride continued beside ours.

"Next time come visit me without your women!" the tavern master called before slamming the door.

Gran was right, I realized as we mounted our horses, about the power of our female presence. It would have been more dangerous for Daddy Asher had he come to this place alone tonight, among people who called themselves good Christians but who had once owned him.

I saw a purple vein appear on the side of Daddy Asher's face. Gran did, too. "Still the great bully, that man is," she said softly.

"Oh, Ginny," my grandfather breathed as he touched the rose-colored silk tie wound through Gran's bound-back braids. The vein receded, and a gust of wind blew his blue-black hair off his shoulders.

Our next destination was a hastily called family conference in the pine grove between our big house and my grandparents' cabin up the hill from it. We'd pulled Susannah from her duties in Freehold, and she'd insisted we ask Gran Constance and Mr. Steenwyck, our elders, to join us. My parents, leaving Jane in Gerald's care, climbed into the grove last.

I poked at the small fire Aunt Susannah had built to ease Mr. Steenwyck's arthritis from the damp air as they spoke of Kikoyo and Ham and Delsey going downriver to that dense, teeming city of New York, then lost forever out of Natchez or New Orleans.

"Only you can get Mr. North's shipment over these mountains," Gran reminded her husband. "I think Josh should go downriver."

My father looked stunned at first, then he smiled. "All right, Mama," he agreed.

"Josh knows nothing about tracking a slave coffle," my grandfather insisted.

"How well could you track your way around New York City, Daddy?" my father challenged him hotly.

"And on what business will you say you're taking your leave from your court duties, Justice Woods?"

My mother's graceful form stepped between her husband and father-in-law. "The Chases and Griffins both desire my husband to prove his loyalties to his oath of office and to the new law. It's a good time for him to be away from here. And it's a good time for Lily to undertake this task with him."

My eyes widened in stunned surprise.

"What?" Daddy Asher demanded.

Even his son moved toward his side of the discussion. "Sarah, I don't think—"

"Don't think, both of you! Listen to me, now that I've managed to distract you from your ages-old, silly bickering!"

"Bravo, Sarah," I heard Mr. Steenwyck say under his breath beside me.

"Nathan and I agree we need a tranquil, quiet haven in which to work toward helping Jane heal herself," Mama continued. "I will ask my relations to leave, and we will quarantine the house." Tears welled in her eyes as she looked at me. "Lily, please understand. I love you with all my heart. But Jane needs me now, as your father needs you. Will you consent to go?"

"I will, Mama." I almost echoed my father's words.

Daddy Asher touched Mama's shoulder in warning, then fanned his fingers out from his lips, hushing us all. He gestured toward the winding, pine-needle path leading up to the pine grove. Instinctively, we— my mother, two grandmothers and I—covered our mouths with our hands. Daddy Asher almost smiled as he beheld our single gesture. "A woman," he predicted of the approaching rustle. "Alone."

In seconds, a panting Mrs. Kearney approached through the high grass of the meadow beyond the clove.

"I beg pardon," she said. "The girl down at the big house said you were gone away. But I saw your fire, heard the voices. Heard none of your talk, though, and wouldn't be listening if I did!" There was fear in her voice, fear bred in the town—about the Woods people being lawless vigilantes serving out their own form of justice.

Mr. Steenwyck stood and held out his hand. "Welcome, good woman." He offered Hugh's landlady his place by the fire. "Rest yourself." She threaded her way through my family members and allowed our courtly Mr. Steenwyck to make her comfortable. When she saw me, her eyes lost most of their remaining fear.

"I promised I'd make a delivery to Miss Lily, and came as soon as I could manage." She searched in her apron pocket until she found the object. She placed a familiarly shaped package in my hands. The paper wrapping looked much worse since the last time I'd seen it—almost as bad as the letter Hugh and his sister had carried across the Atlantic. What did that boy have against paper?

Aunt Susannah touched my shoulder. "What is it, Lily?"

"A present Hugh gave me."

She squeezed my shoulder, then cast a superior look toward Daddy, her twin. He had enough humor to roll his eyes in mock consternation.

The package opened by itself in my lap. But while my relatives admired the gold comb, I stared at the wrapping paper. "There's something written here," I breathed.

Gran pulled her spectacles from her pocket. Mr. Steenwyck leaned over my shoulder, looking down through the lower lenses of his bifocals.

"Hmmm, careful, Lily," he urged. "Looks to be scratched in a very rudimentary manner," he said in his schoolmaster's voice, "with a burnt twig, most likely. It's how our Asher would complete his assignments when the Chases wouldn't spare him a writing implement."

I pressed the many folds as flat as I could and lifted the comb, sweeping it hastily through the hair above my ear. We all seemed to hold our breath together as we looked down at the cinder streaks. The letters were large and clear.

Gwan N.Y.
peer 43

"Peer," Gran said softly. "I think he means pier—where ships are docked, Lily. Hugh leads us!"

"Not Hugh," I said, still staring at the scratched-over paper. "This is how the children say 'gone.' In Delsey's hand. I know it from her slate."

"You must work with those children on their spelling, Lily," Mr. Steenwyck advised. "But the numbers are well formed."

I looked up into my elder's bespectacled eyes. "But why did Delsey write this at all, sir? Why didn't Hugh?"

"Because he cannot, child."

"Cannot?"

"Hugh's illiterate, Lily. It has been my experience that no boy can resist Homer halted in the middle. He did not continue the story himself because he could not. And as reading usually precedes the ability to write, so I doubt he has any knowledge of that skill either."

"But how is that possible? Mrs. Delaney could read and write."

"Ah, Lily." My grandfather's schoolmaster sighed. "Not all families are as fortunate as this one, each generation leaping higher in book learning than the last. It seems to me that famine has blackened the Irish of Hugh's generation to silence."

"He tried to tell me," I realized, remembering his frustration when I showed him the letter telling of Jane's thirteen students, and when he was surrounded by the volumes in our library. And he was fascinated that Ham and Delsey were beginning to read and write. He was trying to be my third student, up in the branches of the white birch tree. Why hadn't I gleaned it then?

"Bright Hugh," Mr. Steenwyck proclaimed, "finding a way to get word of their destination back to us! There's hope for the boy!" He looked over us all before speaking his mind again. "Go downriver with your father, Lily. Bring them all home."

13

FAMILY SECRETS

I sat beside my father in the fore section of the steamboat *Lark*, bound for New York City. There were no other boats leaving that early out of Catskill, so we did not have to listen to the runners, rough men who stood on the docks and tried to get travelers to board their employers' boats instead of the opposition's. With the river trade overcrowded for almost a decade, steamboat owners were desperate for passengers. The shouting between the runners was terrible. I'd even seen a fistfight break out among them once. I was glad our predawn ride to Catskill had freed us of this ugly part of trips to Albany or New York City.

"Warm enough?" Daddy asked as I pulled my mother's bottle-green shawl about my shoulders.

"Oh, yes. I'm just getting closer to Mama's scent."

I could feel his smile as he snuggled me closer against his side.

"Now I know the reason your grandfather finally agreed to our going, I think," he said.

"Why?"

He touched my nose with a gloved finger. "He discerns I'd get lost without the company of an experienced tracker like himself."

"Oh, Daddy." I laughed, tucking my best kid slippers up under me on the bench. "I could hardly track anything in this dreadful dress!"

"Now, now, it was most generous of your Griffin cousin to outfit you as a proper, rich city lady. Though I had to look twice to be sure it was you coming down the stairs on her arm. And that was not because I have need of spectacles, yet."

My ironed curls bounced out of the confines of Wilhemina's stiff hat and brushed his waistcoat as I sighed. Why did in-fashion clothes conspire to keep folks from feeling the warmth of the people they loved? I suspected even my lawyer father did not have an answer to that question, so I asked another.

"Are you angry with Gran and Daddy Asher for telling me of their helping the slaves escape north, Daddy?"

He looked around us on the vessel's second-tier deck. I'd already seen to it that no one was within hearing. Although some of the passengers had seated themselves behind the stack's black fumes, most were in the splendid, enclosed salon. None but ourselves had ventured out in the direct breeze as we steamed down the Hudson at an astonishing twenty miles an hour.

Satisfied, my father sat back. "No. I suppose it was time. They kept that knowledge from me a good many years, you know. They're good at secrets, those two."

"Years? They've been helping Mr. North for years?"

"Since . . . well, since before you were born."

"Truly?"

"Yes. It wasn't even called the name given it now—the Underground Railroad. It was just 'the road,' with trails and paths leading to every notion of hiding areas, from secret places in houses, barns, and haystacks to welcoming tree limbs, swamps, and caves."

"All of which our hills have in abundance."

"Yes. And we're at a crossroads to Canada. North through Plattsburg to Montreal, or west toward Buffalo's border. My father claims I started the association, by inviting Mr. North and his kin to seek their newly freed livelihoods in Stony Clove. The more of the Widow Webber's freed slaves settled in our valley, the more suspicions arose that they were harboring fugitives. Raids began on their small community. One night, before we built Mama's cabin, when we were all still living in the big house, Mr. North made a desperate call. Mama and Mrs. Delaney were enjoying an evening tea. Neither thought twice about shoving a runaway boy into the storage space beside the big kitchen hearth."

"The priest hole."

"What?"

"That's what Hugh called it, from such spaces they used to hide persecuted priests in, in Ireland."

My father smiled. "No wonder the spot came so readily to the mind of his kinswoman. Well, the trackers broke their way in despite my mother standing in the doorway declaring there were no slaves there."

"Did she, Daddy?"

"Without second thought that it was a bald-faced lie, for she had been reading a religious tract about no one being a slave in that sacred spot, his soul. Mama's good at forcing her moral ideas into the practical realm.

"That was the beginning of the alliance between our families," Daddy continued. "Along with Mr. North, my parents know the folks who run the next stations, one twelve miles west, the other almost twenty miles north. That is all they know, because secrecy is why the lines to Canada remain open and grow in number. The Chases have been suspicious of our involvement for years. And they're sniffing closer."

"They were at Daddy Asher's heels tonight," I agreed. "Garret and Parslow both."

"Now, the waterway, that's Ross's and Charlie's specialty. We, or rather, some members of this family, myself always excluded because of my position in the courts, help out from time to time there, too. But mainly we're of use to the land stations. My sister's hid a few families in haystacks and cornfields, I know that much. Mr. North guides both north and west, depending on the hardiness of the passengers. I'm glad you know what I do now, Lily. And I think that's all of us accounted for, or no-accounted for, depending on your stand on slavery: we Stony Clove Woods people, our Steenwyck uncles. I suspect our western wilderness kin will be opening a trail north soon enough." He shook his head. "Renegades all."

"And today we join them."

Daddy grinned one of his unexpected grins that burst forth from his habitually serious face. "Yes."

I squeezed his arm. "And there are many more of us than the Griffins and Chases combined!"

"Does that bring you comfort, Lily?" he asked softly.

"Of course! But not for you?"

"No. Not when I think of losing any."

"Like the Chases lost all their women?"

"Women?" He looked a little lost suddenly, as his eyes drifted over the Hudson's waves to the eastern shore. "Sometimes Chase women could be as mean as the men."

"Like the one you were with at the widow's house? The night you hunted the rabid wolf together?"

"You want another story out of me, Lily Woods," he chided.

"I do. What happened to that one, Daddy?"

"I don't know. She went south to New York."

"New York City? Where we're headed?" I asked in alarm. I didn't like the idea of New York City Chases.

"That was years ago. Rebecca Chase tried to bring my father down when he was indentured to hers. Then she worked her wiles on me. She allied herself with the Griffins, who offered me the education I sought if I'd betray the family."

"How, Daddy?"

"The same way the widow does now, with Jane. By declaring them unfit, insane."

"Daddy."

His jaw clenched in his effort for control.

"We won't allow it, will we?" I whispered.

"Good Lord. This is not a surprise to you. They have spoken to you of it?"

"Yes. I love Jane, Daddy! Mama's right, isn't she? Jane needs our care, not one of those places with whips and chains that she herself used to rail and write letters about?"

"Of course she's right, little one. Jane will stay in our care until she's well, ease your mind about that." His hand formed into a fist. "I will never be crafty enough to predict their next scheme," he whispered.

I covered his fisted hand with mine. "I'm glad of it, this inability."

This coaxed a half smile from him. "I suffer that ancient kinswoman of your mother badly, I know. But that is the root of it, my time as their guest when I was your age. I hope you will not judge me harshly in my hospitality toward her, Lily."

"I think you are the most understanding man on God's earth, Justice Woods."

There. Another of those grins appeared. "It gave me great pleasure to offer Mr. North and his family a place near us years later, I can tell you that. He was good to me that night the Griffins' talons dug deeply into a frightened boy. As good as the ferrywoman who crossed me back over."

"Did you really win us Daddy Asher back from death's door when that ferrywoman came for him the night he was bitten by the rabid wolf?"

"What a notion! Who—"

"Your twin."

"Susannah. I should have known. Lily, listen to me now. My father was very fortunate to have survived his fever. But it was not rabies. The people of Stony Clove like the story so much that they forget rabies does not come on directly after contact. It was a fever my father suffered, brought on by his blood loss. And I did not bargain him back from heaven. He survived because it was not his time, that's all."

"Had Daddy Asher died that night of the wolf, I would have missed knowing him altogether."

My father smiled sadly. "You're getting all the family secrets out of me, little girl," he said. "Now, kindly tell me one of your own."

"My own, sir?"

"Yes. About the purpose behind your recent clearing of new paths over the mountain in my father's company."

I feigned an innocent expression. "Purpose?"

"A new trail connecting with ones leading to Plattsburg and on toward Canada, perhaps?"

"My elder chooses the activity we undertake while passing our time together. I'm not in the habit of questioning it, I enjoy his company so much."

"Spoken like a lawyer's daughter, Lily Woods."

I grinned wide. "Daddy, have I helped pave the way for the delivery of more people north?"

"Shipments, please. We call them all that because one desperate young woman and her two brothers actually came to us inside a crate Charlie Steenwyck smuggled up the river, supposedly containing one of Mr. Cole's paintings for my mother's gallery."

"No! Truly?"

"I had to wrangle the story out of my sister, but have you known your father to indulge in falsehoods, Lily Woods?"

"No, sir. That's why you're the keeper of the family's respectability, I wouldn't wonder."

"What? Is that my role?"

"That's what Daddy Asher says."

"Well." He sighed. "It's been a heavy burden, though I'm the only one of my siblings suited for it, I suppose, stuffy old man that I am and have always been."

"Oh, not to me, Daddy. You are fine and true and upstanding, but not without a touch of the wild, I think."

"Well. Thank you, Lily." The pleasure in his face tempered. "I think." He sighed. "I have a longing to know the whole of it," he admitted, "all the outlandish escapades my mother has penned in those books of hers."

"We share that longing, Daddy!" I said with unbridled glee.

His boyish curiosity disappeared again behind a mask of propriety. "At the same time I hope she keeps the volumes under lock and key until the world is safe for them, of course."

"Of course," I agreed, trying to imitate his sober expression but giggling at this notion of my wise, kind grandmother hiding her lawbreaking past between the covers of her lavender-scented notebooks.

"Daddy. In bringing back Kikoyo and her little ones . . ."

"Yes?"

"You won't stop at legal means, will you?"

"No."

"Then, as you've been entrusted with Gran's estate, it could be the ruination of us all, couldn't it?"

"No trial will ruin this family, Lily. Or dishonor the hills where we dwell," he promised.

14

NEWS OFF THE DOCKSIDE

I felt like a kite about to take flight in my stiff clothes, but I tried not to embarrass my father as we disembarked from the *Lark* in New York harbor. On the dock a slightly disheveled-looking man in clerical black stood with his arms outstretched in greeting.

I leaned into my father's side. "Daddy, how did Uncle Charlie know we were coming?"

He frowned. "My mother is well acquainted with Mr. Morse's invention, Lily."

"But the nearest telegraph office is in Albany! How could Gran possibly—"

"That only she and her vast network of admirers know."

"Or maybe another network. One that carries messages as well as people?"

Uncle Charlie caught me up in his embrace. His dancing eyes crinkled just like Gran Constance's as he leaned forward to give Daddy a hand to grasp.

"Well, Josh, I hear you've left your hallowed corridors for a little city excitement."

Daddy frowned. "This is no game, Charlie," he insisted.

"Oh, but it is. A dangerous one, to be sure. But a game in which your calm, reasoned thinking might be a liability."

I expected anger from Daddy at our uncle's words, however lightly expressed, but to my surprise, he grinned. "I'm only the anchor," he confessed ruefully. "It's Lily will bring this family home, if there's a chance in hell of it. Reverend Lawbreaker," he added ruefully.

I didn't know whether to be more astonished by my father's blasphemy or by his view of our aim, so I just gave myself over to joining in the laughter that burst between two men as opposite as I could have thought possible. As the second son of Gran Constance's marriage to Mr. Steenwyck, Uncle Charlie was close to Daddy's age, and they'd been brought up almost as brothers. Though he had not lived in our valley since he went off to Harvard Divinity School, I often thought Uncle Charlie took his wild childhood home inside him, even over his sojourn serving the poor immigrants of the New York City slums.

"Lily," he interrupted my thoughts, "you look well-to-do enough to get your purse snatched in my neighborhood!"

"Not while I'm in your halo of light, Uncle." I reminded him of his esteemed position, even among thieves.

He laughed. "And in the presence of my glow, you'll require these." He reached into his vest pocket and brought forth a worn case containing wired spectacles shaded the same dark green as Mama's shawl around me.

"Why, Uncle," I said in surprise, "I do not require—"

"Oh, but we require you to look frail as well as wealthy. Put them on, if you please."

I did so, and the teeming bustle of the steamboat landing grew subdued and shaded.

"Very good. Now, if Beatrice can dull those healthy cheeks with rice powder and train you to walk more slowly and lean on your father's arm—"

"Charlie, what is this all about?" my father demanded.

My uncle turned to him. "Why, it's about a sickly young lady who has had Kikoyo North as her trusted companion for seven years now. Her need is desperate, and her beloved, very wealthy father is frantic for their servant's return."

"But . . . none of that is true."

Uncle Charlie frowned, and turned to me. "Lily, have you not visited with Mr. North and his family?"

"Often, sir."

"And when the academy your mother helped found refused to allow the growing children of that community of free persons of color to be taught there, did you and your sister Jane not offer to teach all who were excluded because of their race, among them numbering Kikoyo North's two children?"

"Yes."

"Now, would it be a great stretch of the imagination for you and the young mother who encourages them in their lessons to be called companions in your efforts?"

"No, but—"

"And Lily, have you been well every day of your existence, never requiring the tender ministrations of your mother or grandmothers or Uncle Nathan?"

I had to think a moment on that query. "I had a stomachache when I ate too much berry pie at Daddy's and Aunt Susannah's birthday celebration two years ago, sir," I remembered.

"There! Splendid! So: you have been ill, and Kikoyo North is your companion. Now kindly tell your father that truth is easily gleaned within our slight mechanizations!"

"Daddy?" I quietly appealed to his worried countenance. "What do you think?"

"I think your uncle missed his calling. They could have used him wheedling the last pennies from widows and orphans in old Chancery Court."

Uncle Charlie laughed and put his arm around my father's shoulder. "No, nephew. I'm in the right calling, and exactly where I belong. Many thousands have come up through the port of New York, with many creative bends of the truth serving a higher Truth. I will be the first to rejoice when our mechanizations are not necessary. When it is no longer a sanctioned act to rob and sell people against their will. But that day seems further off than ever in this era of compromise. Preservation of the Union is a noble cause. But we cannot compromise our way out of slavery, Josh," he said. He leaned closer. Even with the lively commerce around us, I heard his soft, sad words: "And I shudder for the children."

Once we arrived at the small stone dwelling next to Uncle Charlie's downtown church, I basked in the warm attentions of my aunt Beatrice and cousin Austin, who, at eighteen, had his mother's dark eyes but was the partner of his father in righteous passion. His admiration of our "mission," as he called it, strengthened my resolve. When I told him of Hugh's message, of Delsey's written note, he donned an old, patched coat and ran off toward the piers that ringed the lower end of Manhattan Island. I envied my cousin this freedom, this ability to blend into the teeming crowds of working people, Wall Street brokers, and sailors along the docks.

Austin's younger sisters, Christina and Lucinda, helped me secure my disguise as a fashionable young lady with fresh attention of their curling irons and the loan of their mother's pearl and garnet earrings. Uncle Charlie sipped his coffee in silence. My father paced around me. As she patted my too-healthy cheeks with her rice powder, Aunt Beatrice hummed a nervous little tune, the same one her sister hummed when Uncle Nathan went visiting patients deep into the night.

"I still don't understand why we cannot merely attempt to purchase Kikoyo's and her children's freedom, Charlie," Daddy insisted. "I have my mother's permission to draw out funds—"

"Because this is not the purchase of a bale of wheat or cotton or even one of your father's horses, Josh."

"Isn't it? To them who send their bounty hunters for our neighbors in the middle of the night?"

"No," Charlie said, quietly countering my father's anger. "The slaveholders are not monsters, Josh, though they sometimes do monstrous things. Now, sit and listen. This is what we have learned. Your neighbor, Kikoyo North, is also Phoebe Custis, a long-ago runaway house servant of Fair Meadow Plantation in the Tidewater section of Virginia. The master of that plantation did not expend great effort or expense to get Phoebe returned. But he is now dead. His son, William Randolph Custis, is master. It is he who has gone to great pains to get a young mother returned to his family. He's spared no expense in his endeavor, as you've already gleaned from the reward offered. And his personal fortune is almost a match for your mother's, Josh, so this is not a problem with a simple, priced solution."

"We need to know his heart," I said slowly. "We need to learn the whys."

My father turned to me. "Whys?"

"Why he wants Kikoyo back so badly," I explained. "Why his father did not. Why Kikoyo and her mother ran away. If only we could talk to her. If only we could talk with him."

Cousin Austin came flying through the doorway then, grinning. "You can, Lily. He's here."

Uncle Charlie and my father turned together.

"Here, son?"

"William Custis has come up from Virginia?"

"It's all over the dockside. From the slave catchers celebrating, and in their cups. Paid off by the master of Fair Meadow himself. He came up the coast in the most beautiful clipper ship I've ever seen. It's called *Atlantic Sovereign,* and it's harbored right where Lily's note said it was—Pier Forty-three."

"And what of Hugh?" I asked anxiously. "Was there an Irish boy among the slave catchers celebrating, Austin?"

"No, Lily. I'm sorry. I found no sign of him among them."

"Daddy," I beseeched, "perhaps if we looked ourselves—"

"There's little time," my cousin warned. "The *Atlantic Sovereign* is due to set sail at first light."

15

BEFORE THE *ATLANTIC SOVEREIGN*

M y father's hand felt cold in mine as our hired cab rode over cobblestone streets slicked by a steady drizzle. I strained to see through it, the descending darkness, and green-tinted lenses before my eyes. I was so far from my mountains, from my grandfather's side. What was I doing here? Work I'd been raised to do, I told myself. Work my family had been doing for many years already. The people of the Woods had risked their lives and Gran's fortune to help strangers bound for Canada.

Delsey and Ham and Kikoyo were not strangers. I could call their sweet faces to my mind in a moment, as I could Mr. North's burned, suffering one. Kikoyo and her children were his family, not the property of the man who owned a beautiful clipper ship. William Randolph Custis. A southerner. Not a monster, I had to remind myself. A man.

Once we arrived at our destination my father opened the cab door and let himself down, then helped me out. He walked us past the driver, who stared. He did not know what to make of us, I thought—doing for ourselves in a city full of poor people making their living by waiting on the rich. Daddy reached up behind the ears of the black gelding who'd pulled us to the waterfront. He rubbed vigorously, eliciting a playful nod from the horse and a smile from the cabman.

"Come. He's gentle, Lily," my father urged.

I stepped forward, enjoying the feel of the withers under my fingers calling up Daddy Asher's horses, and home.

"Remarkable, sir," said the cabman, whose lean frame reminded me of Mr. Steenwyck's.

We both turned. "What's remarkable?" my father asked.

"The young lady. Finding my horse straight off! From your voice, from the smell of him, then, is it?"

The spectacles. He'd thought me blind. The blush rode up my father's neck and ruddied his cheeks. "What's his name?" he asked, quickly turning back to the horse.

"Jack, sir."

"You look tired, Jack."

"Been a long time on these streets," the cabman offered. "Old Jack ain't much to look at these days, and way past his prime. But he's gentle, as you say, sir, and faithful."

"You treat him well."

"Well as I'm able. He returns the favor, and helps us feed our little ones besides, Jack does."

My father nodded. "We wish to retain your services for the length of our visit aboard the *Atlantic Sovereign*." He pulled a crisp new note of currency from his wallet. "Will this suffice?"

The cabman's eyes went wide with surprise. "Oh, nicely, sir."

Daddy glanced up at the sky, which was now pouring down a harder rain. "I don't know how long we'll be," he explained, apology in his voice. "Is there a place nearby where you and Jack might rest yourselves?"

"Yes, sir—a ale house with stable just up the street. Don't fear for me and Jack. Or for yourselves neither. We'll take an hour's meal, then keep a sharp eye out for you both. All through the night, if need be." His eyes skimmed my face shyly. He gasped in surprise when I returned his smile.

"Thank you." Daddy held out his hand. The cabman hesitated, then swiped his fingerless gloved hand across his waistcoat and took it. He searched my father's face before he spoke. "You ain't from around here, are you, Squire?"

Daddy flinched at the title. "Not squire," he corrected gently, "Woods. Josh Woods, and my daughter, Lily. Mr.—?"

"Larson, sir."

He smiled. "You're quite right, Mr. Larson. We're from upriver, mountain country. Does it show?" he asked.

"Mightily!" The cabman laughed, then sobered quickly, surveying the dockside. "There be some rough sorts around after dark, Mr. Woods. You'll look after yourselves, won't you?"

"We will indeed. Thank you."

The cabman lifted his battered top hat and led the hackney cab away. The world around already felt a rougher place without him and his Jack providing a way though it.

"Slowly, Lily," my father instructed as we walked down Pier Forty-three. "Those workers have already caught sight of your . . . remarkable abilities." He put my hand through the crook in his arm. I leaned against him more than I would have without my imagined infirmities.

By the last light of the glowing lanterns set out along the pier, the long, sleek body of the *Atlantic Sovereign* came into view through the misty fog. I counted eight crewmen loading crates and barrels over its shining brass-and-mahogany railed side. Though its sails were all down from its tall masts, it was easy to see from the ship's capacity for them, and its narrow hull, that this vessel was built for speed. I'd seen clipper ships smaller than this one sporting around the steamships on the Hudson, defying the newer power of locomotion on the waves.

My father must have been equally fascinated by the *Atlantic Sovereign,* for he flinched in surprise as two of the workmen jumped over the coiled ropes on the dock and approached us. The bigger one, a full head taller than Daddy and almost twice as broad, adjusted his wad of tobacco deeper into his jaw before he spoke in a hard-edged drawl.

"You should not have sent away your cab. Away with you, you're too late."

"Too late?" Daddy asked, confused.

"Aye. Madame Bourbon's cornering your market now."

"Madame—?" my father repeated.

"Our gracious captain is sealing the deal for us seamen later tonight! They'll be a party in her grand salon, with oysters and dancing and—"

The crewman beside him tapped his shoulder. "This girl ain't no lightskirt, Mr. Ryan," he said, "And he's a gentleman, look at his boots!"

We all took a long second look at each other. Then Daddy started over. "My daughter and I would like to see William Custis," he said.

"You friends of the captain?"

"No."

"So you're wanting to speak on a matter of—?"

"Business."

The man crossed his thick arms. "All of Captain Custis's business is done." He spat a stream of juice that almost left its filthy stain on my skirt's hem. "Yankees," he added, hurling the name like an insult.

"Ask them if they're Quakers, Mr. Ryan," his mate urged now. "You know, come for the . . . cargo? We're to be on the lookout for meddlesome Quakers. Captain says we can throw them in the drink if we'd like."

Ryan shook his head. "Ain't Quakers. Dress too fancy for Quakers, and we can see the girl's hair. Pretty hair. You part of your father's business, gal?"

He reached one finger toward the curls spilling from my hat. Daddy blocked his way. I peeked over his shoulder in time to watch the bigger man step back. Daddy's fierce face. I'd seen it only a few times in my life, that look Gran said he'd come to by way of Daddy Asher, who had it, too, when any of us were threatened. Daddy must have shown his fierce face to the giant dock man to cause his momentary retreat. Red-faced, the man glared at my father now, his general distaste for us turning to something worse.

"No, he's no Quaker. And his nerve comes from being armed. I can see the weapon's place. No nigger-loving Yankee gentleman brings his daughter to the waterfront unless he's armed. Does he, sir?"

Behind Ryan, I heard murmurs of approval. This was how he was saving face, by claiming that a weapon, not Daddy's fierce look, had set him back. The crates and barrels stood idle. All the loaders were forming a circle around us. My father stood his ground, and, though my knees shook beneath my hoop and six petticoats, so did I.

"I am not armed." I heard my father's calm, clear voice.

"You'll allow me to make certain of that," Ryan said, waving the approaching sailors back. "Just me, Yankee," he taunted, drawing a long-bladed knife from his own belt. "I know where you're hiding it." He turned the sharp side of the blade out.

"Step back, Lily," my father whispered.

Did I not move fast enough? Is that why he turned, to see me obey him? When he did, Ryan lunged for his middle. Daddy neatly darted out of his way. His opponent skimmed past my skirts and slipped on his own tobacco juice's slick streak. He came crashing into the wooden planks of the dock. This silenced the men, and made Ryan rage. He gave out a strange, high-pitched yelp before thrusting his knee into my father's middle. Daddy made a stunned, surprised sound. I saw the flash of the big man's blade as Daddy fell to the dock. As I dropped to my knees beside him, a puddle of blood was already staining the planks of the dock and my skirts. He did not move at all.

16

MADAME BOURBON

M r. Ryan!" a voice like a clarinet with a broken reed summoned. "Is chivalry dead? Will no one escort . . . Oh, my, my, my, my, what's this? An altercation?" The voice became a bassoon as it lowered with interest.

I was grateful to whoever owned the changeable voice for clearing the crewmen back from where I held my handkerchief against my father's wounded chin. I replaced my hand with his and yanked open his cravat. "Breathe, Daddy," I urged his startled, unfocused eyes. They reminded me of Ham's when he fell out of a great oak's lower limbs once. "Come on," I urged, as I did Ham on that occasion. "With me . . . that's it, in . . ."

"Ouuut," he groaned softly on his exhalation.

I laughed, so happy that he was breathing again, then caught myself. "Your ribs. Does it hurt to breathe?" I asked.

"Sore only," he assured me. "Lily—" He lost his thought when the crowd descended, led by the owner of the beautiful voice, a woman in a velvet cape. Daddy scrambled to protect me, but his effort caused blood to spatter across his opened cravat and shirt. I gathered the handkerchief against the cut, but blood seeped though my fingers. *Head wounds bleed more.* I heard my two grandmothers' voices join Uncle Nathan's in my mind, keeping me calm.

"Not a step closer, madame!" Ryan warned. "Not before I disarm this filthy abolitionist!"

I only had time to fling my arm across my father's chest before

Ryan's knife descended again. It made a cruel vertical slit across Daddy's waistcoat, opening it.

"Don't worry," Ryan told my horrified eyes. "I only draw blood"—he nodded at my father's cut-open chin—"when I wish to."

His big hands descended, and pulled out the silver case resting where it always did, between my father's shirt and waistcoat, below his heart. He worked its delicate clasp impatiently and flung it open. The sailor's triumphant expression changed when he discovered the box's contents: three ribboned locks of hair and a five-inch oval miniature of Mama, Jane, and me. He flung it down at my skirts so hard a hinge broke. There it rested, opened.

"I . . . I saw the gleam of metal," he offered weakly as his fellows murmured their disapproval—of his actions this time.

"Your master's visitor is formidably armed indeed, Mr. Ryan," the woman called, flute laughter in her voice as she retrieved Daddy's treasure, "with tokens of affection from three ladies, who—" She stopped herself abruptly and raised her lantern to the small portrait painted on ivory, then to Daddy's face. As she did, the lamp illuminated her as well.

Swaddled in folds of lace and deepest red, she was haloed by the strong scent of orchids. There was something unreal about the woman's face, from the bright, almost glittery blond of her elaborately dressed hair to the luminous pallor of her skin, to the artful curves of her dark, shining lips. Painted. I'd heard of women who painted themselves, but never seen one this close.

Suddenly, eyes behind heavy lashes warmed with remembrance. "Why, Joshua Woods!" she exclaimed. "Still taking on opponents much too big for you?"

Daddy squinted in the lantern's light. "Mrs. Elliott?" he whispered.

"No one has called me that name in a quarter century. I am the very exotic Madame Bourbon now, if you please."

"Yes, ma'am. Madame," he amended.

That made her smile. "Well. It's good to see you quicker-witted than last we met, if tilting against no less impossible a cause. The word on the street was that the Steenwycks had been making inquiries about Captain Custis's very private business up the Hudson. But I hardly thought you'd descend from your new judicial duties to . . . Oh, my." Her remarkable voice softened as she looked closer at me, peering past the green tint of my spectacles. "She has your father's eyes, Josh. Is she yours?"

"Yes. Lily. Her name is Lily."

The woman ignored the testiness that had crept into my father's voice, even in our dire circumstances. She offered a silk-gloved hand to me. "Madame Louise Bourbon, Lily," she introduced herself, "almost a member of your family." She cast Daddy a haughty look that challenged him to refute her statement, then added, "By association, not blood, of course."

I took the hand—long, brittle-boned but strong—and tried to speak over my father's low, rumbling growl. "Can you help us meet with Captain Custis, madame?" I asked her.

She smiled, releasing my hand. "Direct. Again, more like her grandfather than yourself, Justice Woods. I am the only one who might perform that miracle, dear child. So kindly urge your father to stop grinding his teeth and remember the lovely teas he once shared with his aunt Rebecca Chase."

"Chase?" I almost yelped.

She put a long, gloved finger to her lips. "Madame Louise here, remember, sweetling? I see your sire carries on the family tradition of driving terror into children's hearts at the sound of Chase. How very tiresome."

Daddy's eyes hardened further as he held out his bloodied hand to her for return of his possession. Madame Louise glanced over it once more, then spoke softly. "They said you married her just to pique the fire of the Griffins. It's not true, is it?"

"No," he answered, his voice finally free of anger. My mother had done that, freed his anger to dissolve into the night air, by the thought of his love for her.

Madame Bourbon closed the broken box gently, then glided it past his waiting hand and into mine. She laughed. "Here, Lily. For deep in your side pocket, as your father seems to have run out of holding spaces in his present ruined state. Button up as best you can, Josh. You'll be on your own once I get you inside. I do hope you know something about these infernal clipper ships, as that's William Custis's sole object of conversational interest besides"—she gave me a quick glance—"besides the subject he will be gentleman enough not to mention in your daughter's presence."

✿　✿　✿

With Madame Bourbon leading the way, my father and I were soon seated in a tiny anteroom of the *Atlantic Sovereign*'s cabin chambers. I took advantage of the bright whale-oil lamps and the clean cloths and water provided by a disgruntled Mr. Ryan to minister to Daddy's wound. All color had drained from his face, and his eyes reflected his fight to remain conscious.

"Has it stopped, Lily?" he asked again, his voice worried about the blood loss weakening him further.

"Almost," I tried to assure him, pressing harder on the cloth. His eyes shut tight against the pain.

"More than a nick of the skin," I heard the soft voice intone behind me.

I turned to see a man who appeared still shy of thirty years staring at the bowl of bloodied water. Daddy opened his eyes in surprise as the sailor touched the cloth I held against the wound. "May I?" he asked us both.

I looked to Daddy, who nodded slowly before I gave up my place. The man's dress was like the other crewmen's, duck trousers and a billowy, cotton muslin shirt. But he wore a blue vest embroidered with trellises of rosemary over his shirt, and was much cleaner than his shipmates—even his hands, the fingers of which were long and graceful and bore only a single swollen bruise around a knuckle. He approached, then lifted the cloth so gently my father did not even wince. "Your daughter's washed the wound well, Mr. Woods. And the pressure has gotten the blood's flow down to a trickle. I can latch the skin together with a few stitches, if you'd like."

Daddy and I exchanged nods. "Please, sir," he agreed.

The sailor glanced at the bloodied water and the stains on Daddy's neck cloth and shirt. "Thirsty?" he asked.

"Yes."

He looked to me. I saw that his eyes were the same color as his vest. There was something about the lean shape of his face, the slight, stubborn thrust of his jaw that was familiar. "Miss Woods," he interrupted my thoughts with his drawl, a softer one than Ryan's, "if you enter through the doorway behind me, you'll find a blue bottle of apple cider set out. There are stemmed glasses in the cabinet below. May I ask that you bring them so your father will have a reward waiting after his travail?"

I looked to Daddy, afraid to leave him with even the ship's courtly, gentle surgeon. "It's all right, Lily," he said, and said something else with his eyes: Go further, if you can. Explore.

But the small provision room where I'd been sent, though full of compartments and drawers made with care of polished hardwoods, had no other door. I walked into its recesses and listened. Nothing but the gentle lap of the waves against the sides of the ship. Where were Kikoyo and her children? Was Hugh still among them?

I found the bottle and glasses and reentered the anteroom, tempted only momentarily to listen beside one of the three doors that led further down and into the ship's cabins. Daddy was lying down on the bench where we'd been sitting moments before, the surgeon already pulling his thread through skin. Had I been gone so long? I set my load down quickly, took my father's hand, and pressed it against my cheek.

"I see my list should have been longer," the surgeon said without looking up from his work, "or the room more interesting. Is your daughter faint of heart, Mr. Woods?"

"Not Lily." Daddy came to my defense as if the man had challenged my honor.

He squeezed my hand. I wondered who was comforting whom as the surgeon tied his neat, swiftly rendered stitches closed. "You can say owww again if you'd like," I said, pushing the sweat-drenched hair back from his forehead.

"No need," he whispered, with only a slight tightness in his voice. "It was not so bad as that."

I helped him sit up. The blue-vested man handed us each a glass of the apple cider. He raised his to my pale father. "To your health, sir," he offered.

Daddy smiled, touching rims. "And to yours, William Custis," he returned the toast.

17

CAPTAIN CUSTIS

At first I thought my father's head injury had addled his wits. How could this handsome, soft-spoken sailor be the dreaded, family-stealing William Custis? But the knowing look between the two men told me it was I who'd been addled.

"Well, since the brilliance of both our disguises has turned diamonds to paste, perhaps you'll allow your daughter the full use of her sharp eyes?" Captain Custis asked Daddy with a sad smile with which I, once again, felt already acquainted.

"I . . . I'm sorry, Daddy," was all I could think to say in my astonishment.

"There is no need for apology, darling girl," he said, hugging me to his side.

William Custis stood abruptly at the sight of our open affection. He paced the small room, running his hand through wheat-colored hair.

"You are not who I expected might come," he said. "Stiff-backed Puritans or Quakers wanting to send them to Africa, or some coarse factory master."

"You are hardly our idea of an enemy yourself, sir," my father conceded.

The captain stood over us, that half-smile lighting his features again. "Well. Come inside. You need rest. Surgeon's orders. I can offer you that much."

We followed William Custis through the rounded double doors and into a spacious sitting room that maintained the sleek lines of his vessel.

"Is this ship your own design, sir?" my father asked the man who had somehow become our host.

"Yes. My twelfth. The *Atlantic Sovereign* hearkens back to the *Chesapeake Sovereign,* a small Baltimore clipper which won every race she competed in on that body of water. I expect this one to do the same in its designated arena. We'll move on from there, my ships and I." He leaned forward. "But I would hardly expect a railway man like yourself to have an interest in ships, Justice Woods."

Daddy smiled, only his eyes showing surprise about how much this man knew of us. "It's my mother who's entitled in the rails."

It was Captain Custis's turn to be surprised. "Your mother, sir?"

"Yes. And since she's had uncanny investment instincts all her life, none of her more formally educated children have been foolish enough to question them. But no family property will interfere with my admiration of the grace and speed of clipper ships. Lily and I first saw one while visiting my wife's Canadian cousin who now lives in East Boston. Remember, Lily?" he said, inviting me into their conversation.

I ceased my scan of the doors and small scratching sounds beyond. "Yes. *The Flying Cloud.*" I looked up, struck again by the captain's familiar profile.

William Custis set down his glass. "*The Flying Cloud?* Did you meet its builder?"

"Meet Donald McKay?" Daddy rejoined. "Why, that's the fellow we visit in East Boston. My wife's kinsman from her first marriage."

"I have admired Donald McKay's clippers all my life, sir!"

"And he should see this vessel. Allow me to write you a letter of introduction for your next voyage to Boston."

"I would consider that—" Captain Custis raised his eyebrow suddenly, his enthusiasm dissolved by distrust. "Why would you do that?" he demanded.

"Because you should meet."

"You seek to serve your purpose, Justice Woods."

"That's true," Daddy said in his matter-of-fact voice before he turned to me. "But the two men would enjoy each other's company in any case. Can you envision it, Lily?"

"Cousin Donald would admire your ship, sir," I offered quietly. "And he speaks of them from the same wellspring of passion, I think."

William Custis leaned forward. "What else do you think, Lily Woods?" he challenged in his soft drawl. "And why do you stare at me?"

"I—do not mean to stare, sir," I stammered. "I have been brought up better, but I remain a most unfinished and artless person, to the despair of my parents and educators alike. Do I not, Daddy?" I begged my father to intercede between me and this man's sharp scrutiny. But it descended in full force.

"You wish to have a servant whose hands are rough and reddened with work returned to do your bidding!"

"Sir?"

"You want me to give up Phoebe!"

I stared at him, confused, until Daddy whispered, "Kikoyo, Lily."

"Her name is Phoebe Custis," her master insisted.

Daddy's voice remained even, measured. "That is not the name she chose for herself among us, Captain."

"Chose! Did you choose your own names? What is this foolishness? Which of us chooses the destiny of his birth? Did my Phoebe live among you, Lily? In your own house, perhaps?"

"No."

"As neighbor."

"Neighbors, yes. Beyond the clove, like us. Their cabins built around Mr. North's forge."

"Her husband was not a blacksmith, but a common day laborer!"

"His father is a blacksmith, sir," I said quietly. "That's the man to whom I was referring."

"Oh. Oh, I see."

"The slave catchers had to beat Mr. North back to get Kikoyo from him, sir. They burned him with—"

"There are communities of free blacks in Virginia, too," the captain interrupted me. "Poor, segregated, barely keeping food in their children's mouths on hardscrabble farms or doing the meanest jobs in towns. Degraded, curfewed, not allowed to bear arms." He whirled on my father. "Is it different in the North, sir?"

"Not substantially, no."

"This woman you have known, has her life been easy?"

"No."

"So. She has had a taste of freedom. A seven-year taste. It's time for her to come home. She will be a house servant again. Her hands will not roughen with lye soap. Her youth will not be robbed with bearing too many children. I promised her all of this."

I considered his words. What I would have before that moment thought an impossibility became possible. "Does Kikoyo desire to go back with you, sir?" I asked quietly.

His light eyes went watery. For the first time, his voice faltered. "She . . . Phoebe does not know what she wants, what's good for her in this time of, of bodily disruption. But I know what is best for her, for those miserable, howling children."

"What's best for whom, Captain Custis?" my father asked, "For them, or for you?"

"You don't understand. How could I expect you to understand?" He began pacing the stateroom.

"Be patient with us, sir," I asked. His pacing slowed, and I dared to delve further. "If her life was good with your family, why did she and her mother run from it?"

"That is none of your concern!"

"True," my father agreed. "But they made that difficult, dangerous choice, Captain Custis, one that millions more have not. They did run."

"It will not be that way again. He's dead! He can't hurt them anymore!" He turned from us then, and stared out the small porthole, his back straight, unyielding. Was he regretting his outburst?

"Your father hurt them, sir?" I asked quietly. "When he was their master?"

"My father, yes. But it was because of me, because I didn't understand. That's what led to all of this." He stared up at the slice of sky through the ship's porthole and hit the brass railing with the side of his fist. "I'm trying to make it all right again for her. Why will she not allow it?"

He turned from the stars to me, as if our common sex could make me know the answer he was desperate to obtain. My hand sought my father's for strength. It was there, and took hold. "Tell us," I whispered.

"I was not the heir to Fair Meadow; my elder brother was. My mother died soon after my birth. As a younger son, I had more free-dom, a longer leash. I grew up, an indulged afterthought always, play-ing beside the servants, then working beside them, to their rhythms, cadence, laughter. I grew up with Phoebe, became . . . became fond of her, when we were about your age, I suspect, Lily. That's when I was packed off summarily aboard one of my father's merchant ships and she and her mother were scheduled to be sold downriver. We were both to be sold off, then, weren't we?

"I didn't know Phoebe and Iris had escaped north until my first leave home three years later, when I'd fallen in love with the sea, with ships, and they had finally given my life some purpose. What had the time given Phoebe? I was forbidden any knowledge of her and her mother. When I persisted in trying to find them, I was finally told why. Told who she is."

Looking at his sad, suffering face, I finally connected its familiarity to the person I knew. "Your sister," I whispered.

"Yes. I have condemned my own sister to the life she's had since a boy's ignorant, misplaced affection, when his few stumbling kisses caused her such misery. Now that my father and brother are dead and I am master, I wish only to bring her home, to make it up to her, to give her and her children a good life."

"She has done that for herself, Captain," my father said gently.

"In your mountain community, sir?" he challenged. "Where even your family, with all its wealth, power, and education, is looked down upon because of the savage antecedents in your bloodline? What has my servant's life been like in your glorious free North? Slaving for wages for you and a host of indifferent masters? Seeing her husband felled in his prime at dangerous work given to only dispensable nig-gers?"

My father looked stung. "I cannot dispute the truth in what you say," he answered quietly. "But it is not the whole truth. There are seven years in the life of a freewoman named Kikoyo North. Consider them. There are children born free and a grandfather who fought like a wolf to keep the slave catchers from taking his family away. And look into your own heart, sir. Were yours the only truth, you would not be in such misery over bringing your property home."

"Is that so? And what do you advise as my alternative?"

"Allow me to purchase this family's freedom."

William Custis leaned forward. "With what? One of your mother's railroad lines, perhaps?"

"You may name your price, sir."

"Price! Property! That's all you northerners understand. Fair Meadow is my home and kingdom, Justice Woods! And that woman is my family! I have a clear, legal right to claim her, and if you ever try to interfere I will see you and all of yours brought down!"

In the vast silence that followed William Custis's thunder, the soft cries and tapping against the smallest door echoed. He turned abruptly and eased it open a crack—enough of a crack to see the glint from Hugh Delaney's coal-black hair.

"I told you your wages depend on your ability to keep them quiet!" Captain Custis whispered impatiently.

"Aye, sir, but the little fellow is sick, you see. And his mam and I are fair worried on it."

"They were not to leave their quarters. You must—"

But by that time Ham had slipped from Hugh's arms and under William Custis's long legs and was bounding toward us. Once the doorway cleared, Delsey followed, and they both landed on me at the same time.

"Why, Miss Lily, you got yourself hoops 'neath your skirts, just like some grand lady!" Delsey said with a shock when she felt the unfamiliar barrier.

"Never mind them," I urged, lifting them both to my lap and returning their hugs.

"Delsey did up the lettering," Ham proclaimed, "but she let me cipher the four and three. I did them right, didn't I? That's how come you found us!"

"You did exactly right. I'm proud of you both."

"Why you crying, then, Miss Lily?"

"I'm . . . happy to see you."

"Oh. That's all right. Long as that man ain't hurt you." He cast a growling countenance toward William Custis. "He can have his rock candy back, his sweet cider, too! He makes Mama cry. I bit his finger," he announced proudly, "clear to the bone, for making my mama cry!"

"You mustn't do that, Ham," I whispered.

"Why not?"

"Because Captain Custis is not a mean man. And he would not hurt you."

"Who is this girl to them?" I heard William Custis ask in a startled whisper.

"Their teacher," Hugh told him.

"Teacher?"

"Aye, sir. Lily Woods is one fine teacher. Not that Delsey and Ham ain't bright lights themselves, of course," he added with a shy, skittering look in my direction. "Them children can read and cipher both. Do sums, too."

"Abilities that I believe are against the law for them to learn in your part of our country, Captain Custis," my father added softly.

"I do not come from your country, sir. I am a Virginian," William Custis countered.

At the sound of Daddy's voice, the children slipped off my lap and presented themselves to him. Delsey did a small curtsy before her hands fisted at her hips. "Why, Mr. Justice Woods, you look miserable stained! And you ain't all buttoned up neat this evening!" she said in surprise. "Mama says you was born right buttoned and proper!"

Daddy fingered his shredded vest. The sides of his mouth twitched in his effort not to laugh.

"Well, I think you look fine, sir." Ham scowled at his sister and offered his hand.

My father shook it. "Thank you, Ham," he said. "I feel considerably less than that."

"You and Miss Lily come to bring us all home, sir?" Delsey asked him then.

"That's . . . that's why we've come, yes, children," Daddy said so softly I thought my heart would break with the sound. He rested his hand on the little boy's head and drew him against his side.

"Fetch their mother, you cunning Irishman," I heard William Custis's hard voice order Hugh with a growl.

18

KIKOYO'S PRICE

Regal. That was the word I thought of as I watched Kikoyo stand before us. She'd placed her bare feet far apart to accommodate her late, low-slung pregnancy. Her blue cotton dress was tattered but her favorite red striped head cloth freshly wound. The face beneath it was swollen but dry-eyed, even after the children sprang from my lap into their mother's arms.

William Custis turned away from the sight of another embrace, but not before the resemblance between himself and his sister locked in my mind forever—from the stubborn thrust of both jaws to the graceful purpose of their hands, one roughened by washing, one by manning sails. A black finger wore a wedding band, the white, a nephew's bite.

Kikoyo raised her solemn eyes to ours. "How fares Daddy North, the rest?" she asked.

"Recovering, all," my father assured her. "And you?"

"I am most grateful to your daughter, sir, for putting her young man in charge of our care."

I looked to Hugh, whose eyes asked mine not to protest Kikoyo's understanding of his place among her and her children.

"He has been our defender among the cruel men who first held us in captivity," Kikoyo continued in her slow, measured, correct English, the likes of which I'd never before heard from her. She had not trusted us with her ability to "speak properly". And why should she? "While here," she continued, "Mr. Delaney has kept my children in good cheer. And myself from the depths of despair with assurances of your arrival."

"Please. Sit," William Custis told us all tersely.

We all did except for Hugh, who stood against the wall, near where he'd allowed the children to escape his care. Was he guarding or protecting his charges now? How did Captain Custis regard him after Kikoyo's pronouncement that I'd sent him as their protector? Was he angry? Did he think Hugh had betrayed him? There was no telling from the captain's light eyes, which had gone hard and unyielding of any thought or feeling. Only purpose remained, as hard and bright as a stone shining up through the water of Batavia Kill. Who was this man? I wondered again. My own circle of watchful protection expanded to include one I knew better now—Hugh, his own changeling grey eyes exhausted but watchful for a means of rescue.

Captain Custis addressed his sister, though she had not once looked at him since she'd entered the cabin.

"Phoebe."

She stared straight ahead, giving no acknowledgment of her slave name. Captain Custis's jaw tightened before he continued. "These people have convinced me that your children might be better off not being . . . disrupted from the life they've known. So I offer you a compromise. Though I am as fully their master as I am yours, I will allow Justice Woods and his daughter to return the two children to Stony Clove, on the condition you promise no resistance on our journey and no attempt to escape from home thereafter."

I found it difficult to breathe in the silence that followed, especially as I watched Kikoyo's dark eyes spill tears. When the children saw them they knelt up on the bench beside her.

"You hear? We going home, Mama, don't cry no more!" Ham insisted.

But Delsey stroked her mother's face, asking, "What does he mean? Mama, what does he mean?"

Kikoyo pressed each head to her shoulder and rocked her children in silence.

Daddy stood. "This is a compromise conceived in Hell, Mr. Custis," he said in a white-hot voice I'd never before heard from him, even in his worse arguments with Daddy Asher.

"Do not fling your Yankee fire and brimstone at me, sir! What else have all the compromises between our countries been?"

Kikoyo raised a hand so like her brother's, silencing their argument. She turned to William Custis for the first time. The glassy hardness of his eyes shattered with the look she gave him.

"Write it down," she said.

"What?"

"My children's freedom. Write it down."

"Phoebe, I give you my word as a—"

"Justice Woods will witness. Mr. Thomas North, a free man and their grandfather, will be their guardian. And I will kill you stone dead if ever you change your mind and send your slave catchers for my children, William Custis."

Her enflamed eyes released him then, and she went back to the care of her babies. My father approached Captain Custis.

"There," he said, "master of Fair Meadow. You have found her price. Do you enjoy playing Solomon?"

"No," the master breathed out, anything but triumphant.

When he stood, I fought the urge to feel more sorry for William Randolph Custis than for his beautiful, weeping sister or for the children.

Captain Custis left us then, closing the cabin door softly behind him. He did not return.

Kikoyo spoke softly to her children, then put Delsey in my arms and Ham in Hugh's while she sang them an African-cadenced lullaby. If the mother of these children could do that, who was I to indulge myself in grief? I felt Delsey relax against my heart with the soothing sounds of her mother's voice. She slept. When I glanced at Hugh I saw that Kikoyo had achieved her purpose with Ham, too.

"They are good children," she told us softly as we set them out together on the cushioned bench. I placed Mama's shawl over them both. "Good, sound sleepers, too. Not troublesome. Daddy North knows that. My children will make him proud. They will be—"

The soft tap at the cabin door jolted all of us except Kikoyo's children. The painted woman stepping into the cabin held the hastily drawn-up pack of belongings in one hand, the fine-grained leather folder in the other. Again I felt tongue-tied in her presence. "Madame," was as much of her names as I dared pass my lips, along with a small curtsy.

She handed the pack of clothing to Hugh and entrusted the folder to me. As Hugh made a pillow for each of our charges with the clothing, Madame Bourbon's eyes lingered on him. She gave me a knowing smile. "Finely formed," she said approvingly before she faced my father.

"It seems your eloquence has won the day again, Joshua."

He stared hard at her. "You need not mock me, madame."

"I?" She placed her hand to her bosom. "I have never possessed the wit to mock. I speak without irony." She stared at him. "You don't believe me."

"I learned that long ago, madame."

She released a skittering, girlish laugh into the cabin's gloom. "So cynical you've become, Joshua. I suppose I shall have to allow these papers to speak for me. If you'll hand them to your father, Lily. To peruse only. Store them in your pocket, dear. He has little capacity for carrying anything tonight except the family pride and an interesting scar."

My father took the folder from my hands. As he read through Captain Custis's dense, black handwriting, a grin of delight suddenly freed his sullen features. He rushed to Kikoyo's side and knelt. "He's changed his mind," he said.

"Good Lord, he covets us all again?"

"No, Kikoyo. He's signed free papers. For all of you."

"Are you sure, sir?"

"Yes."

Her hand rested on the bulge below her heart. "The baby, too?"

My father pointed to the place on her document. "See here?" he explained. "It says 'all future issue.' That's what your new baby is, future issue."

Kikoyo let out a whooping call that I thought would bring the timbers of the cabin's low ceiling down before flinging her arms around Daddy and hugging him hard enough to make him gasp in the pain it caused his sore middle. She backed away, stroking her long hands over his arms as she went.

"I beg your pardon, Mr. Woods!"

Daddy only laughed.

"Bless you, sir," she exulted in her more familiar, African-influenced cadence. "Bless you and your whole mighty family!"

"We are blessed many times over," Daddy whispered, glancing at me, Hugh, and the still miraculously sleeping little ones. "But it was not us. You caused this, I think. You and your lullaby finally touched the man's soul."

Madame Bourbon stepped forward, annoyed, I thought, at being left out of our celebration. "Captain Custis asked me to sign as witness," she said with distaste. "That should be a plum to take home to your renegade father, Justice Woods."

I looked over Daddy's shoulder to where her long, polished nail pointed on the document. "*Rebecca Chase Elliott,*" it proclaimed in a steady hand.

"Our families can't seem to rid ourselves of connections, can we, Josh?" she asked softly.

"No, ma'am," he said, the respectful boy again.

"Keep your guard up. Both Griffins and Chases will be after your mother's treasures till all the seas go dry."

"Yes, ma'am," he said, sounding tired. "I expect so."

She shook her head. "Well, I'm to see you to the dock, where your faithful cabman awaits, threatening to bring the constable down on all our heads if we've harmed you."

My father hesitated, glancing back at the cabin door. "Captain Custis. Mrs. Elliott, should I—" The woman who'd been Phoebe Custis stepped up beside him, a measure of guarded concern in her eyes, too.

"No. Leave him to me, now, chicks," Madame Bourbon advised. "After failing with you, Josh, I lowered my sights. Damaged young men have become my specialty."

Outside, the rain had stopped and the stars hailed down close in the summer sky, reflected again in the water. The crewmen eyed us watchfully, some of them muttering on the eccentricity of their captain's decisions. But most watched Madame Bourbon's bright skirts slicing through her cape.

She took my father's hand in hers once we'd all walked to the dock. "You will tell him I am still beautiful?" I heard her whisper. "You will grant me one little lie among your sea of almighty truths?"

It was only then I realized that applying "beautiful" to the Chase who had refashioned herself a Bourbon was a lie, that the woman before us was made beautiful only by her artifice and the cloak of night.

My father nodded. "I will tell him your beauty went beyond the . . . uh, splendor of your surface," he promised.

She took his shoulder and pulled him down to receive her kiss on his cheek. "They did teach you something at Harvard. Sweet liar," she said, leaving a smear of bright red where her lips had touched. Another scar, I thought, with an interesting story I would get out of him someday, about this woman who still loved my grandfather.

19

THE THIRTEEN

W e need to get home," Kikoyo insisted again. "I can't stand the thought of Daddy North worrying."

"But you and the children also need to rest," my father said quietly. "Ah, Beatrice. Too tight," he warned his aunt as she swaddled his middle with the strips of cloth Kikoyo and I were heating on the iron of the cookstove. She loosened it, and his breathing eased.

"We can send a telegram, Kikoyo," I offered. "The operator in Catskill will ride out to Gran with it."

"Won't be enough. He needs to see us. Got to start. We'll find our way, don't you worry about us."

Her long strides were taking in the length of the small Steenwyck kitchen in three steps, despite her low-lying burden.

"Nesting," Aunt Beatrice said quietly. "It won't be long."

"Long? Before what?" Daddy asked, startled.

"Come now, Josh," she chided. "You haven't been at court during all the birthing times in your family, have you?"

"She's . . . that close?"

"And glowing."

"Glowing. I remember my sister's times and, yes, Sarah glowing, just before you were born, Lily." His eyes warmed as they went from the steaming, mint-scented cloth in my hands to my face. Then those eyes panicked. "We've got to get home, then! What's keeping Charlie and Austin? When does that blasted night ship leave?"

"Hugh," Aunt Beatrice summoned, "I might need your help in keeping my patient still."

Hugh rose from his place beside Delsey and Ham, asleep against his side on the parson's bench. Kikoyo whirled on Aunt Beatrice before he reached his destination. "Do you have help, Mrs. Steenwyck?" she demanded suddenly.

"Help?"

"With the housekeeping—cooking and cleaning and all."

"Why, yes."

She turned to Daddy now. "You hear this good lady, Justice Woods? You see how small this house is, put up against your place? How can you burden your missus with it all, sir?"

Daddy stretched his hand over his eyes. The small glass of Madeira Uncle Charlie had insisted he drink before we started the treatment of his bruised muscles had eased his body but dulled his wits. "I'm afraid I'm not following," he admitted in confusion.

"Of course you're not! What do the menfolk know of anything but counting houses and courts and horses and taking their pleasure with—oh, I beg your pardon, Mrs. Steenwyck."

Aunt Beatrice laughed. "Do speak plainly, Mrs. North. I rather enjoy our peerless Josh being browbeaten."

"Beatrice!" he protested, wincing, "don't encourage her."

"Sit still, or you'll do yourself harm. Open your mind to what this lady is saying, child!"

"I'm less than three years your junior, Aunt. I will not have you either calling me child or encouraging this woman in her pursuit of— just what are you in pursuit of, Kikoyo?" my father asked, confused again.

When faced with his direct inquiry, Kikoyo went suddenly silent. Hugh yanked his curls back from his brow, that nervous gesture I'd grown to love, and approached my father.

"My kinswoman's place beside your hearth, sir?" he began quietly with one of his soft questions. "Seems to me it needs filling, aye? It's a big estate, yours is, and you're a man of some importance, whether you like it or no. And your mother didn't leave you the place to let it become a burden to your lady, sir."

"Burden?"

"Listen to the boy, Josh," Aunt Beatrice encouraged. "Have we not been telling you that it's a hardship for Sarah to manage the big house without help? Not to mention Susannah and her family, whom you call in on the occasions of entertaining. And there's keeping the gallery, and the library, and—"

"But we're Woods, Beatrice," my father whispered. "We don't have servants. What would my father say?"

"Your father welcomed Mrs. Delaney into your household."

"But Mrs. Delaney, she was . . ." His hand passed over his brow again. My poor father looked so tired. "She was family."

"Open your eyes, Josh." Aunt Beatrice nodded toward the children under Mama's shawl. "This night you've lost a bucket of your life's blood, acquired a notch in your chin, and taken a pounding your middle regions will be weeks forgetting. For your mighty principles alone?"

"No."

"That's good. Because this lady and her children are bound to take your efforts very personally all their lives. Now, would you have Kikoyo continue an unhappy toil that keeps her from her children's side, or join your household helping your good and gentle wife?"

Hugh grinned, crouching before Daddy. "And would you think how fast those two little *babs* and the one to come would learn their letters if they lived in the same house with their teacher?"

Daddy frowned. "And how much easier that teacher would be for you to locate, Hugh Delaney."

"You slander me, Mr. Woods," Hugh insisted with a wounded look. "True, I wouldn't have to climb trees to get a look at her. But your daughter is a fierce woman on her own territory. If I'm displeasing her she'll be flinging me down each of your mighty mountain peaks in turn, I'm thinking."

My aunt opened her eyes wide. "You must allow me to make you a pot of good black tea, Mr. Delaney," she said.

"Your upstate sister already has, mum." He cast a quick glance at me. "The leaves she studied in my cup afterward pleased her enough to lend me her woman's guidance. How else have I gotten the little ways I have towards my heart's desire?"

Kikoyo approached us again with those long, even strides, the last steaming cloth over her arm. Daddy touched the hand she pressed over his aching middle.

"Would you and your family consider accepting a place with us, madame?"

She raised shining eyes to Aunt Beatrice. "We would indeed, sir. And we would never give you cause to regret it. Or the cookstove."

"Cookstove?"

"Daddy North can pipe it in on the side chimney, sir—the one that holds the Dutch oven. He's done it in all the cabins in Freehold. So you can still have your open hearth as well. But you got to pull yourself into this century, Mr. Woods; it's halfway gone! You'll get used to the sight of it in your ancient kitchen. And you won't regret the cookstove any more than my children and me, not when you taste what I can make up on it!"

"I—don't know how Sarah will feel about a cookstove . . ."

"Oh, you leave your good lady to me, sir. Your daughters as well. Once they get to baking and boiling on my cookstove, they'll wonder how they made do without it."

"Well, then. I will talk to my wife on—"

"Oh, I've done that already, sir. Months past, when I lost my good man. She said you're the tough nut to crack in this."

"She did?"

"Yes, sir. Done, then?"

Daddy closed his eyes against all our broad smiles. "Done, madame," he agreed. "But we must build you a house."

"House, Mr. Woods? You got more room than—"

"And land. To leave your children. Your brother will never say I was your master."

"Is that so important to you, sir?"

"It is, madame."

"Than I will buy both from you, sir. Out of my wages."

Kikoyo took Uncle Charlie's shirt from my hands. She pulled it over Daddy's head as if he were one of her children, speaking softly as she did. "Well, now, after I could find the courage to go back into slavery, asking for the place at your hearth became a mighty easier thing, sir. Still, I needed Miss Lily's young man's help, imagine that?"

"Imagine." My father's eyes searched for me. I took his hand and knelt beside him. "How did I get to be a tough nut, Lily?" he asked, his breath soft and sweet with the taste of the wine.

"You are thoroughly cracked now, Daddy," I assured him.

His eyes brightened with a mix of mirth and indignation. "I am weary of being the great respectable example of this lawless family."

"Rest from it," I soothed, kissing his brow, then helping Aunt Beatrice lay him out on the cushioned bench.

"A little while only," he whispered, closing his eyes. "We've got to get them home tonight, Lily."

"Your father cannot hold his liquor," Hugh said as we sat out on the Steenwycks' front porch steps, searching out the sky together.

"He is not used to it, is all," I protested. "We only indulge in spirits on rare occasions."

"Ah, then." He nodded. "That explains its powerful medicinal effects."

"Are you deriding my father, Hugh Delaney?" I demanded.

"Not for the world!" he insisted. "I'm just . . . I've got nerves skittering with being alone with you, Lily, and I'm speaking every foolish thing that comes in my head."

"Why?"

"To keep you here by my side, love."

My heart sang upon hearing his soft endearment.

He stared at his hands for a long time before he spoke again. "Joining up with the slave catchers. Accepting the work from Captain Custis on the ship. I did not do any of it for the money, Lily," he claimed, breaking the silence between us.

"Oh?"

"I mean, it sickened me, the raid on the North forge. It called to mind too much of what I've seen in my own country at the hands of the landlords. And I knew you and your folks wouldn't allow the taking of them, not here in America, the New World. So I saw my place with the woman—with Mrs. North and her children, keeping them well as best I could until you'd get to them, you see? So I told them you sent me, to ease the way for them, even though it was the last thing you might have done, considering how last we parted."

I touched his rolled-up sleeve. "I wish it were true."

"Do you? None will hear it called false from my lips, then." He turned away from my grateful eyes and rested his long arms across his knees. "There is something else," he said, his eyes scanning the beautiful comb dressing my hair.

"Yes?"

"The children wrote the note telling our destination because . . . because I can neither read nor write."

"I know that, Hugh."

He turned his head sharply. "You do?"

"I should have gleaned it myself," I apologized. "Mr. Steenwyck had to tell me."

"You know?" he asked again.

"Yes. Your interest in the battle for Troy without turning the page he marked gave you away to him."

"I did not mean to deceive you. I am ashamed, you see?"

"Could Marcella read and write, Hugh?"

"No. None of us younger ones could, on account of the famine and . . . all else."

"You are not ashamed of your sister, are you?"

"Of course not!"

"Well, I understand no reason why you should be of yourself."

He scratched the side of his face. There was no beard there; he must have shaved aboard the clipper ship. "I thought if I stayed in the tree, listening while you taught the little ones," he explained, "that I could try again to learn my letters, and the reading, without you knowing my ignorance. You aren't the English schoolmaster, teaching hatred of my own people along with his lessons. And I don't have the hunger to fight dulling everything but keeping my mam and Marcy and the little ones and me alive from one day to the next and . . . Well, you are the only teacher I'm wanting, Lily Woods," he said softly.

I struggled for breath. "That will be a great disappointment to my elderly kinsman, Mr. Steenwyck," I stammered. "You're just the sort of student who provides a simulating challenge to even his formidable talents. And he'll be trying to steal Delsey away from me, on account of her atrocious spelling."

I could not keep up this dance around the question. I flung my arms around Hugh's neck. "You forgive my misjudgment of you? You will be coming back with us, then?"

"Well, surely, Lily," he said, smiling, "I owe my landlady three weeks on the rent. Did you fancy a deadbeat idler was courting you?"

Our kiss was as warm and sweet as the summer air of our mountains.

"Will you sit upon my knee, Lily Woods?" he whispered as it ended.

It was no easy task in my cousin's finery, but we managed. Hugh circled my bone-corseted waist with his long workman's hands. As we kissed this time, my fingers wove paths through his dense black curls. I felt lost in him, in the power of his goodness and passion that pounded from each beat of his heart.

"Ach, Lily," he laughed. "There won't always be silk and fish bones between us."

"Not fish," I corrected. "They're whalebone. Whales are not fish but breathers, like us."

We both felt the insistent tug at my skirts.

"Your preacher uncle's got our tickets, Miss Lily," Ham sang out happily. "And we got lots of ladies for company, Mama says!"

"Lily, do you still have the green-tinted glasses?" my cousin Austin asked, springing out the door as Hugh set me back on my feet.

"In my pocket, why?"

"There's a shipment could use your company."

"Ship—? Oh, shipment."

"You surely are being christened by fire in your family's courage pool!" he exclaimed with—what was it?—envy in his voice. "The shipment's a strong-willed matriarch and her kin up from Maryland—nine in number. An even dozen with Kikoyo and her children. That's if you get them further along on their journey before they are thirteen!"

"Thirteen?" I repeated, casting a glance at Hugh beside me.

He smiled slowly, his eyes glowing with purpose.

"They have the bounty hunters at their heels," Austin continued. "So we have to move quickly. There is not time to draw up convincing counterfeit free papers, so you must be very careful. We'll split them up between you and your father, so as not to draw attention to so large a number of women."

"Women?" Hugh said. "Women are they all?"

"Yes."

I caught the metallic scent of Hugh's fear as Austin proceeded. "Lily, your father moves feebly enough to need the care of half the ladies."

"Poor Daddy!" I proclaimed. "How will all those handmaidens sit with his conscience?"

"Keep telling him they are temporary servants only, will you? He's as bad a liar as you are."

"Austin Steenwyck!" I protested. "We're new to all this, is all!"

"You must have a care what you say about her father," Hugh advised my cousin, "kin or no!"

Austin frowned. "They're all that way, the Woods people. For your half of our charges . . . Hugh, what do you think of our poor-sighted heiress with weak limbs besides?"

"She's no trouble at all, as light as geese down," he said softly. "You have it from her humble Irish servant."

20

THE FLIGHT OF THE *ARTEMIS*

The scene at the pier was even more crowded than when Daddy and I had arrived. From my place in our hired cab, I saw two steamboats waited side by side at one dock, the *Artemis* and the *Francis Kendrick*. "Do New York people ever sleep?" I asked my cousin.

Austin laughed. "Night boats, Lily," he explained. "It's all the rage to Albany. Unfortunately, so is racing. And I'd say these two might challenge each other."

I followed his nod toward both vessels' captains on their hurricane decks, looking at their watches. A wave of fear made me shiver.

Hugh took my hand. "We'll get home, Lily," he said.

"All of us?"

"The lot."

"You, too?" I whispered.

"Sure, me. Your wild grandfather has promised me an excursion along those peaks that gird 'round your valley. Will that christen me properly into a new American?"

His humor chased away my foreboding. I squeezed his arm. "I'm sure it will."

"There's my father," Austin announced, tapping the cab's ceiling with his cane.

Uncle Charlie was on the crowd's periphery with his part of our "shipment," four huddled, dark-clad women and girls. They did not look very different from the immigrants pouring onto both steamships. The Hudson was a route of heavy travel for thousands going on to Buffalo and the Great Lakes toward western settlement. Surely we would all blend in among them here in the darkness? Hugh lifted me from the carriage. What had seemed like a disagreeable burden on me—my imaginary helplessness—now seemed more a burden on him.

"I pray I remain as light as geese feathers to you through this night, Hugh Delaney," I whispered fondly at his ear.

"No fraternization with the servants," he scolded. "You Woods folks will never know what's proper!"

"Lucky for you."

"Aye," he breathed, giving up both argument and indignation as his nose skimmed my ear. "*Mathair na Dia,* Lily, you're close enough to taste!"

"And I have a powerful desire to be tasted. Are you putting an Irish enchantment on me, Hugh Delaney?"

"Nay," he said. "I'm calling on God's mother's help in keeping me a good Christian man."

I had yet to catch my breath from the curious tingle that our sparking exchange provoked when my uncle hastily introduced Martha Lee, a small woman with strong, determined features, her two daughters, and a daughter-in-law. I was frightened to do much more than nod to each, for by that time our entourage had become an object of interest. And Hugh was right; I had little knowledge of how a highborn lady acted with servants. But when the younger daughter, a girl I judged about my own age, took my hand, I squeezed and smiled, hoping my fear didn't show itself to her, whose very liberty was at risk.

I looked for my father and the others among those crowding toward the ships. "They are boarded already, thanks to Beatrice's gracious, insistent manner," my uncle informed me. "Ah, here she is," he exclaimed, urging us forward to meet my aunt as she pushed her way confidently across the current of boarding passengers.

"Aunt Beatrice is so brave," I admired aloud.

My uncle snorted. "No, Lily. She's just a New Yorker."

She met us, breathless, pressing something in my hand. "The key to your stateroom. It adjoins your father's," she said above the runners' increasingly passionate yelling.

"Airy cabins, gentlemen!" called one.

"Top speed twenty-eight miles per hour!"

"Twenty-nine!" claimed his competition.

Uncle Charlie put his arm around his wife as he spoke to us. "Josh's watching out for you, I've no doubt," he told me, "while we see that all goes smoothly from our place on shore. Go with God. Ladies, Lily, Hugh."

My aunt kissed my cheek. Austin grinned. "And welcome to the family enterprise, cousins," he said.

Hugh's whistle became our small group's beacon through the crowd. Behind us, the women latched themselves on either side of Martha Lee. She had a firm grasp of Hugh's coat. I wondered if Hugh knew the fairy tale of the boy and his goose to whom all who touched were fastened securely. High in his arms I felt like his goose, leading a parade.

I glanced up at the long, sharp bow of the *Artemis*. Her engine used the steam over and over, and so had no chuffing exhaust pipes. Her side paddle wheels and "walking beam" gleamed like a huge iron see-saw above the topmost deck.

On the quarterdeck, a young midshipman holding a wide book watched us instead of the names of each passenger signing in. Why? He smiled and waved shyly when I caught him staring, a bright, friendly smile, making me feel less frightened. Well, we were a sight, I reasoned; why shouldn't he find us amusing?

The rough-edged voice called "Halt!"

Hugh stood stock-still. Then he turned so that our party must have looked like a slow-tailed comet changing course before we faced the seven rough-looking men and their leader.

"I've got a warrant for the return of darkies of their description to Maryland," he announced.

I looked up, panicked to speechlessness. It was a good thing for all of us that Hugh was not rendered so. He planted his feet firmly on the dock and stared the man down. "Look elsewhere," he said evenly.

"After you show us their papers, naming them slave or free." The grizzly-bearded man turned his hard eyes on me and spoke louder, as if I were deaf as well as crippled and poor-sighted. "Maybe you have your servants' papers, miss?"

I finally found my voice. "My father does. He's ill and gone on board already, sir. I'm very sorry. I hadn't expected to be asked for them."

"There! You heard her," a young boy yelled from the crowd around us. "Now off with you, stinking slave catchers!"

"Not without a look at those papers," the head of the slave catchers demanded again.

"Is there a problem?" I heard a man's voice inquire. Hugh turned us to face the young midshipman who had been watching our approach.

Hugh looked at him as if he were the enemy. "Problem? Only if a proper young woman cannot be taken at her word on this ship!" he announced. "If it's so, I'm thinking her father, sick as he is, will be storming over to the *Francis Kendrick* rather than stay to hear his daughter insulted aboard the *Artemis!*"

"Aye, bring the lot of them aboard, lad!" One of the runners claimed his part in the argument. "And all passengers with a conscience that balks at these filthy slave catchers roaming our streets, stealing away folks, should board the *Francis Kendrick!*"

The runners for the *Artemis* tried to shout him down, but others in the crowd were now voicing opinions of their own—varied, contentious, but most siding with our small party. The midshipman held up his hand.

The slave catcher waved his warrant. "This is a right proper document," he insisted, "and the law says . . ."

"What law?" someone behind Martha Lee shouted. "Southern law? This is a free state, in the antislavery camp!"

A few of the slave catchers began to back away from the crowd's increasing menace. Their leader halted them. "Stay where you are, boys! I know my rights! It's a federal law says I can transport stolen property and have these abolitionist thieves arrested!"

Soon neither side could hear the other for the shouting. The very air around us seemed charged with anger. Into the fray a dark-clad man stepped, brushing by me without acknowledgment but with the scent of mint poultice about him. His very presence seemed to have a calming effect on all. I'd seen my father do the same in court, and at the assembly in Albany.

"May I be of assistance?" he asked quietly.

The young midshipman's eyes looked to him with hope. "How, sir?" he asked.

"I'm a lawyer." He looked at the leader of the slave catchers. "May I look at your warrant, sir, to see if it is indeed in good order before any other course of action is taken?"

"It's all proper," the man muttered before handing it over.

My father's eyes scanned it slowly. "Yes, as you say, everything seems to be in order, so I'm afraid this young woman's father may have to bear the inconvenience of producing . . . Ah now, wait."

"What? What?" the slave catcher demanded.

"This warrant isn't signed."

"Signed? By who?"

"A justice of the peace. I'm afraid it isn't valid without that signature."

"Well . . . where's one of them?"

The midshipman's eyes went wide as he glanced down at the names in the passenger book in his hands. He'd remembered my father from the boarding—I could see it in his guileless face. He knew the man before him was Justice Woods, who could sign the document in a thrice. But he said nothing.

My father smiled. "Where indeed?" he pondered. "I'm afraid I'm not native to this area, sir." He lifted his head and spoke louder. "Perhaps one of these good people might—"

"Reverend Steenwyck!" someone in the crowd shouted. "He can take you straightaway to a justice, our reverend can!"

Uncle Charlie stepped forward. "I'd be only too glad to escort you and your party to one, sir."

But the slave catcher looked askance at the suddenly quiet crowd, as if he and his men were the only ones left out of a secret, which probably was near to the truth of it. Finally his eyes beseeched my father. Daddy met their consternation with a benign smile and offered his good lawyer's counsel. "Can any of us do better than with a man of God as guide?"

The slave catcher waved his document up at the *Artemis*'s captain as he stood surveying the scene like a monarch from the hurricane deck. "Official federal business!" he shouted. "Don't go yet! You hear me?"

When the captain gave no sign that he'd heard, the head catcher entreated my father. "Will you tell him, sir?"

Daddy smiled benignly. "I'll convey your message," he agreed. He could look so upright doing so because he hadn't said when, of course.

Satisfied, the slave catchers turned and followed Uncle Charlie through the crowd.

Hugh held me closer. "Without a lie," he marveled. "You and that respectable sire of yours did it all without a single lie. I've been bested, Lily. A hundred generations of Delaney blarney's been bested this night."

The deep sound of the whistle blasted from the neighboring *Francis Kendrick,* announcing the steamer was about to sail. The captain of our own *Artemis* closed his watch and disappeared from the deck.

The midshipman sighed, shaking his head. "Best get the remaining members of your party aboard, Justice Woods," he advised.

21

FOLLOWING THE NORTH STAR

The *Artemis*'s grand salon stood in marked, peaceable contrast to the commotion of the outside. It was two decks high, and lighted by glass chandeliers hanging from the ceiling. All floors and stairways were richly carpeted in shades of blue. People were strolling about or sitting in the many armchairs, talking in hushed tones or reading. Musicians were tuning up their fiddles and horns at one end. The galleries on the deck above held strollers touring the ship's opulent interior.

Daddy led us quickly to his stateroom. There Kikoyo showed signs of her future among us as she pushed him into the berth below the one her sleeping children shared. He took her badgering with good grace, perhaps because he'd always been comfortable with the gruff tenderness of difficult women. I did not do as well when Kikoyo shooed the rest of us through the adjoining doorway.

"Wait," I protested, "I need to tell him . . ."

"What, Miss Lily?"

"That I'm proud of him. That I love him."

"Lord, he knows that! He's asleep on his feet, child. Tell him when he wakes. Mister Hugh, get yourself outside on deck to keep watch for those slave catchers."

"Yes, mum," he proclaimed, eyes lit with excitement.

"I'll go, too," I offered.

Kikoyo scowled at me. "Carrying you would slow him down considerably, Miss Lily."

"But he doesn't need to . . . Oh, yes." I remembered my disguise. Hugh grabbed his cap and kissed my cheek before he disappeared outside the door.

I looked at the frightened, anxious faces of the women in the small room and felt ashamed of my piqued state. I pulled back the velvet green curtain from the stateroom's window. "Look," I urged them closer, "see the stars?"

Slowly, holding each others' hands, they approached.

"The drinking gourd. We still be headed north, sisters," Martha Lee assured them all. "Even over this water."

"Yes, north. The Hudson flows from Lake Tear in the Clouds," I said softly. "Canada's beyond."

"Tear in the Clouds. Pretty name," the girl about my age said.

"Miss Lily, please read these sisters the letter from your kinsman now," Kikoyo suggested.

"All right," I agreed. Martha Lee handed me the carefully folded note in my Uncle Charlie's hand. " 'Lily,' " I read aloud. " 'I have wired ahead to Ross to meet the *Artemis* when it docks at Edwards Landing. He will take charge of your shipment from there. Your family might then ferry over to Catskill, where your faithful horses wait to carry you home.' "

Suddenly, the big gong sounded from the engine room. A shudder ran through the floor and walls around us as the wheels began to turn. I smiled at the anxious faces of the women. "We're casting off, with no warning from Hugh that the slave catchers made it back in time. If I know my Uncle Charlie, he's led them on such a merry chase that the justice who'll sign their warrant resides in Brooklyn!"

"Where's Mr. Hugh?" Martha Lee voiced the same concern that plagued me.

"On his way, I'm sure. Maybe he stopped to watch the engineer at the steam valves hooked up to speed. It's a wondrous operation!"

We turned back to our window on the river and watched the water rushing past below. "Edwards Landing is north of Clermont, on the east side of the Hudson," I explained. "We'll be there before daylight, especially if the rivalry between these two boats causes any racing."

"Racing, miss?"

Behind the women, Kikoyo crossed her arms and frowned at me. "You'll like my uncle Ross." I changed the subject quickly, secure again in telling tales of my family. "He's not as funny as Charlie, but he argues something fine, and can fix about anything that can break! And his wife, Clara, she makes the best pot pie of a Sunday."

"With chicken inside, miss?"

"Great hunks of chicken! And potatoes, carrots, and snap beans—" A slight tap at the door silenced me. I slipped on my tinted glasses and sat as Martha Lee flung my mother's shawl across the wide lap I had with my hoops, all of it making me an invalid again. But it was Hugh alone at the door, carrying a bulging flour cloth sack in one hand and a covered pail of steaming tea in the other. "Lily Woods," he scolded me, "all that talk of great hunks of chicken and potatoes is going to make what I've scavenged up from the kitchen seem meager indeed!"

"Oh, no, sir," Martha Lee assured him. "My gals and me, we got right good heads for imaginings when it comes to food!"

Hugh handed her the sack. "You have that in common with the Irish," he said, tugging on his cap.

I felt such pride in him then, looking over what his merry tongue had procured from the kitchen staff of the *Artemis*—crisp crusted bread, great hunks of cheese, even a small jar of honey. We set some of his bounty aside for my father and Kikoyo's sleeping children, then feasted together. I remember few meals tasting as good as that one.

Hugh and I soon had our guests asleep under blankets we'd found in storage compartments. We sat together in a stuffed chair near the window, where we could watch the stars and hear the sprightly dance tunes ringing up from the band playing below.

"Will you come dancing with me of a Sunday when we get home, Lily Woods?" he asked softly against the hair at my temple.

"If you'll come to harvest and Saint Martin's and all manner of frolics at Community House in my company."

I felt his smile. "Between us, we should keep our feet flying in the years ahead, I'd expect."

"Aye."

I cozied closer and closed my eyes. I don't know how long we slept like that, spooned into each other's sides in the big chair, but the last I remembered the band's music had turned toward waltzes. Then I dreamed my grandfather's horses were screaming. I woke with a start. "Hugh!"

"I've got you, Marcy," he called, his grip tightening. "Lily," he amended, blinking. "What is it, love?"

I touched his face. "I don't know. Something's wrong. I need to see my father."

"All right, then," he agreed, without a word of complaint.

"Mind the ladies," he cautioned as we made our way around the sleeping women in the dimly lit cabin. We slipped into my father's stateroom just as Daddy himself came bounding through the door that led out to the ship's salon. He looked the opposite of the rested man I sought in his berth. His disheveled brown curls fell carelessly over reddened eyes. He stepped quietly past Kikoyo and her sleeping children. I caught the scent of night air and steam about him.

"Daddy," I whispered, "you're supposed to be sleeping."

"The speed. It woke me. Too fast."

My father has inherited Gran Constance's habit of talking in very short sentences when worried.

He took my arm and guided us all to the window. A fog, unseasonable for this deep in summer, was slowly rising off the water.

"Too fast," Daddy whispered, "for this weather. This visibility. We're traveling too fast. In the pilot house. I tried to tell them."

"Who, Daddy?"

"The captain, the officers. None but that young midshipman agreed."

"Why won't they listen to you, sir?" Hugh asked.

A low horn answered. Daddy nodded toward the window. "Look," he breathed.

We gazed down the aft of the ship to see the dim outline of the *Francis Kendrick* approaching.

"The captain won't slow," Daddy said, pulling his hand through his hair. "I last saw Roundout, the port of Kingston. We're approaching Trapp's Reef. Deep channels on the eastern side. A good forty feet. But narrow. It's mad to be racing here, were it good weather. We'd best disembark."

"Now?"

"At the next port. We'll find a carriage. Or the train. Get the women ready. I'll try again in the engine room. If they've tied down safety valves to build up steam pressure—That's it. I'll threaten the engineer with legal action. The boilers are ripe for . . ."

"Explosion?" Hugh prompted.

"Yes."

"I'll join you sir," Hugh offered.

"No, son. You must look after the women, the children. Have them gather their belongings. Be ready to head for the quarterdeck. Calm. Help them stay calm. Yes?"

Hugh nodded. "Aye. God go with you, sir."

I took hold of my father's sleeve. He touched my face.

"Don't go," I pleaded. "Daddy. Your sentences. They're so short."

He kissed my forehead. "You sound a tad worried yourself, darling Lily," he said before he left us.

I stared at the door, fighting the fear that made my fingertips feel icy. Hugh touched my back. I faced him, grinding my teeth, sounding nothing like a student of Mrs. Beech. "Turn around," I ordered.

"Turn around? Why? Lily, we've got to wake—"

"First things first," I insisted, yanking up the hem of my skirt. "I'm ridding myself of the corset and these horrible hoops!"

The hoops were falling to the floor when the two ships collided with a crash.

22

THE WRECK

I was suddenly sprawled against Hugh's chest, with Ham in my lap. The little boy raised sleepy eyes to mine and patted my cheek.

"You two fixing to bed down with us, Miss Lily?" he asked.

Hugh rubbed the side of his head that had hit the room's seaward wall. "No. We're—"

But an explosion drowned the rest of his reply. It shook the stateroom violently. I heard the ceiling lamp crash, plunging us into darkness. I tucked Ham deeper within my skirts even as Hugh's arms shielded my face from the shattering glass and hot oil. An eerie silence descended. I felt suspended between earth and hell.

"Boiler's blown," Hugh said at my ear.

"Daddy!"

"We'll find him," he promised gruffly. "But now we've got to get the women out, like he charged us."

"On the open deck."

"That's right, love."

"I'll help," Ham offered from his place under my chin, "if you'll quit swaddling me in your underwear, Miss Lily!"

From her bunk, Kikoyo summoned her lost child.

"We've got him over here, mum!" Hugh called, the laughter in his voice a settling contrast to the screams and moans we now heard outside the door. "Stay there now, we're coming."

As standing was impossible at the angle the floor now was, we managed, with little Ham between us, to crawl to the bunk still secured firmly to the inner wall. We put Ham in Kikoyo's arms. Hugh leaned over the berth's edge and began buttoning a still sleepy Delsey's blue coat around her, out of habit, I thought, from taking care of them in their recent captivity.

"I'll call the others in," I offered.

"Mind the glass," Hugh warned as I made my way to the adjoining stateroom.

I was easily guided by the light shining beneath the door. "Their lamp didn't break, like ours," I called back. "Maybe their floor won't be all buckled and difficult to—" I swung open the door.

"Sure," Hugh said behind me. "Go on. Lily, what's keeping—" His hand, about to propel me forward, now fisted the silk of my dress so tightly three silver buttons popped, opening the bodice.

I heard his tongue lock at the back of his throat. It found voice again through the port of his first language. *"Dia's Muire agus Padraig!"* Hugh Delaney called on his Irish God and saints for help in understanding what we saw before us: not the second stateroom but a great gaping hole, with a long drop to the fog-shrouded Hudson below. And no sign of Martha Lee and her kinswomen except for a bright head cloth waving from a splintered piece of wood.

I was about to follow them. The ship gave a shuddering pitch. Hugh's free arm swung around my middle, barred the way to my fall just before we were flung back inside. We stood, pinned together against the still secure double berth.

I let go a whimper against forces so much bigger than we were. But I fought the desire to crawl up in the berth beside Kikoyo and her children, a desire born of the notion that it was the only safe place left in the world.

"Can you take Delsey?" Hugh whispered.

I did not respond, still fighting images of the Hudson swallowing women, my father blown to pieces in the engine room, the outside screams of panic.

"Lily?"

Hugh twisted me around. He held me so tight against his chest I felt myself blending into him, past shirt and skin and muscle to the vital beating of his heart.

"Lily," he called. "I need you. Please. Help me."

I nodded. Hugh's arms loosened their grip. His lips pressed fervently against my brow before he released me.

"Delsey," I whispered. "Can you see my hand?"

"Sure." Delsey. Sweet Delsey, sounding just like herself, anchoring me as Hugh's kiss had. "Grab it, that's the girl—one hand for me, the other for your mama."

"Come," Hugh instructed, swinging Ham onto his back as if we were out for a Sunday stroll. "Shall we try the other door?"

When we did the world righted itself again. But it was not the stately world of our arrival. We were swept into a flood of people rushing for the ship's grand stairway that led to the quarterdeck. I smelled—what was it, through all the fear and sweat? *Smoke*.

"Eyes front, Lily," Hugh commanded when I almost tripped over an abandoned carpetbag.

A few feet ahead, the crowd was parting around a little towheaded boy in his nightshirt, holding onto the balcony rail and calling for his mother. Without thinking I scooped him up with my free arm, adding him to our party. He clung nicely to my neck so that I didn't even break stride. Beside me, Kikoyo shook her head and smiled a weary, strained smile. "Miss Lily," she scolded softly, "you and your mama and the babies!"

We caught whiffs of fresh air. It was a blessed relief to see the sky above the open second deck. But we also saw the effects of the *Artemis* being struck by the *Francis Kendrick*. The steamship was hog-backed—broken in two toward the aft. Water poured into the splintered hull. The *Artemis* was sinking and the *Francis Kendrick* nowhere in sight. Could the ship have rammed us and then steamed on? The smoke that sooted the air inside was from a fire I could see now, one that had started in the engine room and was now spreading to the cabins. I said a quick prayer for the people I could see jumping overboard to escape the flames. Lights sparked from a shoreline community, and lanterned rescue boats were casting off.

I directed my attention to our means of escape—small boats being filled with folks and lowered to the water on rope pulleys. I scanned the faces in the first two. The oarsmen were ship's officers, the passengers women and children. I scanned the faces in the crowd.

"Do you see your mama?" I asked the little boy in my arms.

He shook his head, then buried it against my neck.

"We'll find her," I said, trying to sooth him. And myself, for I searched among the coughing people pouring on deck for my father. As the crowd surged forward, Kikoyo pressed herself against Hugh. Her head bowed, her hand taking hold of his arm.

"What is it, mum?" Hugh asked softly.

"It will pass," she answered in a strained whisper.

Delsey tugged my skirt. "What's ailing Mama, Miss Lily?" she asked.

"We're all feeling a little closed in," I answered assuringly. "Do you have your mouth organ, Delsey? That would brighten the spirits of all within hearing, I think."

She smiled. "Captain Custis liked my music, too, Miss Lily—a sight better than Ham's bites, he said."

"Only bit him the once," Ham insisted before his sister started a sprightly tune, one that made Hugh smile.

"Why, you play fair hornpipe, Delsey," he said.

"Is that what it is, sir?"

"Sure."

"I heard it down below us, in the grand dancing place," she said. "This, too."

Delsey then proceeded to play from memory the rudiments of dances that had been ringing out all night—a cotillion, two polkas, and a waltz. Her playing eased the worry of all around us and passed the time.

Kikoyo smiled with pride at her daughter. But she also had stretches of leaning on Hugh and looking lost, pulled away from our place on the deck for minutes at a time. That's when it dawned on me that her baby was coming.

"Hey!" A crewman alerted Delsey when our place in the rescue line had come. "Keep playing, little pickaninny. But over there." He pointed to the aft. He looked at me. "Yourself and the boy, miss," he directed. "We're only taking women and children as of yet."

"But," I stammered, "Kikoyo. Her children—"

"Are niggers. Niggers can wait."

I looked up at Hugh. His arm pulled the suffering mother closer under his protection as his eyes steeled in contained rage. But those dark, changeable eyes also told me any decision I made would be all right with him.

"I can wait, too, then," I told the boatman, and stepped aside. The little boy in my arms clung to me tighter. I could feel the disapproving mutters. But a woman climbing into the boat reached out her arms. "I'll take your brother along with me, miss," she offered.

I nodded, pulling the boy's arms from around my neck. "This lady will help you find your mama," I whispered before giving him over. He blurred from sight as they lowered his boat. No doubt the hot cinders burning my eyes, of course.

Hugh touched my back. "He'll be all right, Lily," he whispered.

Behind us, the fire was being fed by a strong river breeze. How long would they make Kikoyo and her children wait? I wondered. There weren't enough boats, or time. I touched Hugh's face.

"Can you swim?" I asked him softly.

"No."

"Give me your knife," I said.

"What?"

"Your knife, if you please."

He handed it over, and with it I tore strips from the hem of my petticoats.

"Lily, what are you doing?"

"Daddy Asher taught us all to swim in Echo Lake, didn't he, Delsey, Ham, Kikoyo?" I asked.

The children nodded enthusiastically, but Kikoyo's smile was sad. "I'm a mite weighted down for swimming, Miss Lily," she said, gasping and reaching for Hugh's arm again.

I waited for the passing of her pain, thankful that I had not been shunted from my family's birthing room. From my aunts' confinements it seemed to me that Kikoyo was still in the early time of her laboring.

"So you're a little weighted, and Hugh needs lessons. So I'm tying us together."

Hugh frowned. "You're doing no such—"

"Jump, feet first, like we do off Hibb's Point into the swimming hole in Batavia Kill. Yes, Ham? Delsey? Kick for all you're worth to the surface, get some air. Then we'll look for a small craft or wood debris. Together."

"Won't we sink?" The question came from a worried young man listening nearby.

"No," I assured him, "not if you rid yourself of heavy clothes and shoes. And take hold of wood. It will keep you afloat while you kick into the shallows."

"What does she know?" a companion of the young man demanded.

"She's been touched by God, Harry! She's the one come on board blind and lame. Now she's in the bloom of health, rescues orphans, won't even take the boat she's offered."

His companion snorted. "Won't go without her niggers. Maybe she's just plain touched."

Hugh rose to his feet, his arms flexed. "My Lily's a miracle of God's creation," he told the men in a smoldering tone. "And Himself, Padraig, and Blessed Bridget will rise in fury to hear her slan—"

Another explosion rocked the *Artemis*, tilting us all sideways and spilling the lowering boatload of survivors into the Hudson.

Without another word of argument, our companions scrambled to yank off their woolen coats and shoes.

Dense smoke poured out from all doorways. The ship was burning fast down to the waterline. Men scorched black streamed out of the opening nearest to us, collapsing onto the deck. They were burned and bleeding. I looked down at my frayed skirts and petticoats and believed one more could go without significant loss to the maidenly reputation Hugh was willing to defend under any circumstances.

The injured men were patient with my clumsy efforts to relieve their suffering. "Are you boilermen?" I asked as I bound the hand of one.

"Aye, miss."

"My father was going to the engine room before the collision. Perhaps you saw him?"

"The man with Mr. Bingham, both of them ready to take the boat out of the captain's command for his racing? Sounded like a lawyer?"

"That's him!"

"Him and Mr. Bingham, they stayed within when the stack came down on some children, miss," another boilerman volunteered.

"Yanking them up over the broken rail for folks to catch. Fine fellow, your father."

"Did you see him after that?" I pleaded, scanning their faces. "Any of you?"

"We were right busy reversing the engines, trying to keep any more boilers from blowing. Then the stairs come down and—well, we didn't see much of anything after that."

"The captain and hurricane deck officers are coming just behind us, miss. Maybe they know—"

Before he finished, the officers, their smart uniforms now as scorched as the rest of us, barreled through the doorway. I grabbed a tarnished gold-braid sleeve blindly. "Sir, my father—"

"Your father's a damned fool, young woman," he barked at me. "There was nothing I could do. Correct, Mr. Hawkins?"

"Yes, sir," the man beside him affirmed. "He chose his fate when he wouldn't leave Midshipman Bingham."

"No hope for Bingham, of course."

"None, sir, rest easy. You offered the more humane end. Now they'll both go down. Needless."

I flew at the two like a screaming banshee, Hugh said later, though I don't remember raising my voice, only pounding at gold buttons before his strong arms pulled me back.

The *Artemis* gave out a creaking groan. Her death throes. The officers disappeared in the swirling smoke.

"Hugh!" I called above the terrible sounds.

"I'm here, Lily."

"I have to find my father."

"Aye," he grunted. "We'd best go, then."

23

SALLY HAMILTON

Ours was neither the act of lunacy nor bravery that folks made it into later. It was a simple task, made of few parts. There was still a low passageway through the smoke. We took it, groping on our hands and knees. We had only to follow the voices—my father's, a low and soothing contrast to the pained pleading for abandonment from the other.

"Daddy!" I called, willing my scratched and splinted knees to crawl faster.

"Lily! Is Hugh with you?"

"Yes, sir!" he answered for himself.

"Excellent!"

We saw them then, amid the rubble of a ruined stairway, the lower half of young midshipman trapped, my father kneeling beside him. "My family's of sensible stock, Mr. Bingham," he said cheerfully, "and knows there are better uses for a crowbar than mashing your poor brains."

"Poor indeed, to have doubted you, sir," the young midshipman said, then fainted.

Daddy brought my hand against the cold iron of the lever. "Here, Hugh, beside Lily. On my signal, press down with all your strength, while I pull our steadfast seaman from his prison. Now."

We did as instructed.

"More," my father commanded. I remembered working on the road over Second Sister Mountain with Daddy Asher. My strength, unlike Hugh's, lay not in fists and arm muscles but in the simple weight of my body. I did as he bade me—I sat on the bar.

Something heaved, gave way. "He's free!" Hugh proclaimed. The *Artemis* listed to the side, as if reluctant to give up her hold on her last officer. Smoke billowed up around us.

"Let's go," my father instructed, anchoring the young man under his arm. "Lead, if you would, Lily, and we will follow"—his voice suddenly went prim—"what's left of your skirts."

Then it was only a matter of finding that patch of stars showing through the smoke. See? Simple.

Kikoyo and her children, their wrists tied to each other, were waiting for us as we emerged from the burning grand salon.

"Why, Kikoyo," Daddy said with quiet concern as he squatted beside her and the children. "You look a little indisposed."

"I'm managing my burden, Mr. Josh," she replied with a wan smile. "And you look like a relation from my mama's side of the family, sir," she teased, scraping a thumb across his sooted cheek.

"Is our shipment of women safe, gone for shore?"

"I . . . I lost them, sir," Hugh said behind him.

"What?"

"Through the cabin. The floor gave way. Gone."

"All right, son," Daddy soothed with a steady hand on Hugh's shaking shoulder.

I looked over the ship's rail. Small pieces of burning debris lit the water. Calls and crying rang out over the water, but sounds as well as sights were shrouded, indistinct, tricking my ears' efforts to locate them.

I had a strong sense that we were the only ones left on the creaking, tilting deck of the sinking steamship.

Even in the dim haze of the night I could see that our loyal midshipman who had not given my father away to the slave catchers was badly burned along his neck and chest. "Mr. Bingham," Daddy called, shaking him slightly, "the *Artemis* is finally yours to command, sir!"

The young officer's dark eyes opened at the summons. He surveyed the deck and his remaining passengers, listened intently when the ship listed again.

"We've got to jump. Now," he said. "She's going down fast. She'll take us with her."

"Very good, sir," my father answered. Hugh knelt to remove the young man's boots as I began to fashion a muslin line between him and Daddy.

"No," Mr. Bingham protested. "I'll be a millstone to you, Justice Woods."

My father grinned at me. "Lily and I will forgive that insult to our swimming teacher," he said. "Now, don't risk another mutiny this day, son. Let me—"

"Hello the *Artemis!*" The female call came up from the water.

Daddy stood stock-still. Slowly his fingers, bashed and bruised from his efforts to free the children and the midshipman, rose beautifully, almost dancerlike, through his hair to touch his ear. He walked to the railing. "Hello the sloop!" he answered, although I could not even see the vaguest outline of a vessel. "We are seven! Two children, one injured man."

"I have the room, if ye'll jump toward the burning waste straight before ye."

Daddy turned shining, awestruck eyes to me. "Darling Lily," he whispered. "Will you be our lead once more?"

Was this my sensible father, flinging me out toward a voice? Was this myself, calmly taking his hand and the one Hugh offered on my other side, climbing over the rail, jumping?

The Hudson, after the eternity before I hit it and sank deep, was dense and black. I followed my own advice and kicked. I was soon rewarded with a dim view through the water of my burning debris target. My head had not cleared the surface long enough for me to get my bearing before a long, strong arm reached for me. I grasped it and looked up into the smiling face of my grandfather. One even motion had me over the side of a small sloop, as if he was bearing the weight of the child I once was, swinging on his arm.

I heard my father's distant call but could not find my answer as I stared at my grandfather. He was in lightweight homespun trousers braced up over a billowy shirt. Something was fastened to the shirt, over his heart. Something red. It danced there in the breeze. The call again, splintered with worry. Had Gran given him a piece of her hair ribbon before he'd left, for luck? I turned from that token to his face. It had never looked so beautiful to me, and I was struck, lost in it, in his fathomless eyes, the way Hugh had been in Mr. Cole's painting.

"Make your daddy an answer, Lily," he chided me.

I turned to face the dark mist. "I'm aboard!" I yelled out. "We watch for the next!"

Kikoyo and her children took their turn, and all swam skillfully through the dark waters. She realized before I did that Daddy Asher and the hailing woman who now sat at the tiller with a nest of lanterns circling her feet were not the only occupants of the trim, open craft of eighteen or twenty feet. Sitting along the starboard side were Martha Lee and her kinswomen. They passed Ham and Delsey along their line for warming hugs.

"Good catch tonight, Captain Woods," the woman at the tiller approved, her voice rich and full and accented like my mother's. I could not see her face except for the glowing white lace frill at her brow and the shine of her teeth. But she sounded young, perhaps a few years my elder.

"Who's next?" Daddy Asher asked me.

I turned toward the water. "We've got them, Daddy!" I called out.

"Mr. Bingham and I come," he announced before I heard their splash.

"The injured man," my grandfather said.

"Yes, burned."

We gathered Mr. Bingham gently over the side.

Then I had the great fortune of seeing my father stare at his as if Asher Woods was made of mist instead of flesh. "D-Daddy?" he stammered.

Daddy Asher smiled gently. "You invited me on this trim little craft once, remember?"

Daddy looked over the faces of the North family, then Martha Lee and her kin. "All here?" he asked in astonishment.

"All, sir," Martha Lee announced proudly. "Floor fell out with us, all of a piece. We drifted almost midriver hanging on to our floor before this here boat met us, brought us round to you-all."

My father's eyes finally found the tillerwoman. "Daddy," he summoned, "Is she—?"

"Let's get our Delaney aboard, shall we, son?"

Daddy nodded. "Hugh!" he called out. "It's your turn. Come join us."

Nothing. Until finally, quietly, "Too heavy. I'll sink, surely."

I felt Hugh's fear, saw his mind watch his sister's body slipping into the waves of the Atlantic. I leaned over the side of the sloop. "Hugh Delaney!" I shouted. "Jump into this water before I climb up there and push your miserable bones off myself!"

I could feel Daddy Asher's grin. "She sounds like her grandmother," he said.

All further sound was silenced by the yell Hugh gave out as he jumped from the burning deck.

"Hugh!" I tried calling him to the surface. His head emerged just beside the sloop's bow. My father and I each grabbed an arm to pull him on board. He lay, his head in my lap, shivering and panting for breath. His dazed eyes took us all in until the tillerwoman spoke.

"Any closer and you'd have landed in my sails, child," she remarked.

Hugh's eyes narrowed. "*An de bheoaibh no de mhairbh thu!*" he called out, backing away from her and into the haven of my arms.

The woman cast a quick glance at my grandfather, then gave my father her place at the tiller. She took up one of her tin lanterns, punctured with swirling shapes. She approached slowly, then knelt on the deck beside us. I could see her face now, framed by her old-fashioned cap and the flying wisps of honey-touched red hair escaping it. That face had seen suffering, but still bore hope. She covered my hand at Hugh's shoulder with her callused fingers and took up one of Hugh's hands with her other. All chill from being in the dark water left me.

"*Curirim mo dhochas ar snamh i mbaidn teangen,*" she said softly.

They stared at each other. "Trust her, Hugh, she's family," I whispered, though I had no idea of the meaning of the words either of them had spoken.

Hugh nodded slowly. His shivering stopped.

"Good, then," the tillerwoman said. "Help me raise the sails, young ones, so we might take advantage of the great swell left by that hissing contraption."

She sounded so like a typical sloop ferrywoman then, complaining about the steamers hogging the river, that I laughed aloud. But I stopped as the *Artemis* went down to her grave in that deep channel of the Hudson.

Navigating the swell she left in her wake was more thrilling than anything I'd experienced in either steamship or railway carriage. Hugh and I held down the ropes, but it was still like being in the hand of God. As I looked at the placid face of the tillerwoman, at my grand-father and father flanking her like tall sentinels, my mind finally named her: Sally Hamilton, the murdered servant who had belonged to Squire William Sutherland in the century before ours. We were in the presence of our family's ghost.

24

MARCELLA'S SONG

A peaceful silence reigned as the swell finally spent itself. The wind was at our backs as we sailed on through the lifting fog. As the stars reappeared overhead, Martha Lee pointed skyward. "Still north," she assured her kinswomen.

Here, upriver of the devastation and suffering, the water reflected the starry night sky, the western shoreline, and the purple outline of our mountains.

Just before us, lit beautifully by the stars, was a small rounded mass of land, harboring only a few pine and elm trees. Daddy Asher's hand pressed his son's shoulder. "My father spoke of this place," he whispered.

"Aye." Sally Hamilton nodded. "Turtle Island."

"The Mohicans say no one dies there."

"A good place to camp some passengers, Captain Woods?" she asked him.

Daddy Asher looked at Kikoyo and her children, and smiled. He knelt beside Mr. Bingham, lying in the small boat's bow. The ship's officer was moaning quietly. My grandfather took a glass vial from his medicine bag and rubbed a few drops of its contents on his temple. Soon the sloop was scented lavender, and the moans stopped.

"Josh," Daddy Asher summoned, "Ross is waiting across the river to conduct these ladies on north."

"I am charged to deliver the women, sir," Hugh said quietly. "You must stay with your family now."

Daddy looked worried. "But the authorities are sure to be there, too, looking out for Martha Lee and—"

"My handmaidens?" Mr. Bingham asked, pulling himself up to his elbows. "Surely no one will question the rights of a burned officer in the care of his hired servants, Justice Woods? And no one will be checking my poor burned clothing for free papers."

Daddy stroked the hair back from the young man's fevered brow. "My brother Nathan has a friend, a physician whose name and home Ross knows. This doctor will take you in for as long as you need care."

"We'll get him there, sir," Martha Lee promised.

Daddy sighed. "I cannot seem to keep you out of trouble's path, Mr. Bingham."

"I hope this will not prove the end of your efforts, sir," he replied, smiling, as Hugh squired Martha Lee and her womenfolk around their new master for the evening.

My grandfather turned to his son. At that moment I saw more clearly than ever the physical resemblance between the two men I loved best in the world. "We'll wait for Hugh's return on Turtle Island," my grandfather said.

"All right, Daddy," my father agreed, but took his father's sleeve, almost like a child would. "She'll bring him back?" he whispered.

"Oh, yes. She brought you back to us, didn't she? I think Lily has some work ahead, too," he said, staring pointedly at Kikoyo.

"Oh, no, Captain Woods!" Kikoyo claimed, her old fire flaring. "I'm not going to hold anybody up! Daddy North is worried about us. Pains have come and gone. False labor, that's all. I'm having this baby at home!"

"Then allow us to build you a warming fire for your brief sojourn on my ancestors' island, madame."

Her frown melted into a smile, as most women's did under the spell of Daddy Asher's charms. "Well. That'd be right cozy, thank you, sir," she allowed.

So the ferrywoman piloted us to Turtle Island, then, leaving us with two of her lanterns, poled out on the river again. Martha Lee and the women looked after Mr. Bingham while Hugh manned the tiller.

Once they were on the river, the ferrywoman took his place. I watched Hugh fondly as he waved a lantern, smiling the same smile as the taller woman beside him. When he said something at her ear, the woman raised her arm in a greeting I returned. Then she began a plaintive tune I'd never heard before. Hugh picked up her song, and their voices blended beautifully.

> *"The pratties they grow small*
> *Over here, over here*
> *Oh, the pratties they grow small*
> *And they're failing in the fall*
> *Still we eat them, skins and all*
> *Over here.*
>
> *"How I wish that we were geese*
> *Night and morn, night and morn*
> *How I wish that we were geese*
> *For they fly and take their ease*
> *And they live their lives in peace,*
> *Eating corn."*

None of the women in Martha Lee's company were taller than Hugh. I quickly counted heads. Twelve. One too many. I ran to the river's edge but never got a better view of Marcella Delaney.

On our island refuge, Kikoyo rested on the mound of pine needles Daddy Asher had the children fashion to accommodate her shape. Ham and Delsey cuddled up like opossum children beside her.

My father watched over them, looking sad and bereft without his sailor to care for. Daddy Asher and I took one of the tillerwoman's lanterns and explored the small circumference of the island. My grandfather's sharp eyes directed me to plants and flowers. "Ah, there's still some comfrey in flower, see it, Lily?"

We knelt together beside the small clump of deep pink blossoms. Daddy Asher chanted a gentle song.

> *"You are ready with your healing*
> *Now I claim you, take you,*
> *Take you for your healing virtues only."*

We had done this many times together, but now, listening to my grandfather's low, sweet voice and watching his large, scarred hands bathed in moonlight as he gathered made me want to cry.

"Make a poultice of the flowers and leaves," he instructed, bringing me back to our duties, "for any soreness or if there's tearing."

"Tearing, Daddy Asher?"

"When the baby comes."

"Do you think Kikoyo will have her baby tonight?"

He shrugged, looking up at the sky. "The stars are very bright." His eyes returned to their scan of the river's edge. "Look. Raspberries."

"Too early for fruit, sir."

"But the perfect time for harvesting the leaves."

My petticoats took on yet another use that night, as Daddy Asher, singing, plucked fresh green slips to use in making Kikoyo a birthing tea.

"Uncle Nathan's not the only one that listens to Gran Constance and her remedies," I marveled quietly as we approached our camp.

Daddy Asher grunted. "Any man who does not cherish the ladies is a fool, born and bred. I expect Kikoyo's new free man will learn that soon enough."

But rather than enjoying the compliment, as I was, Kikoyo looked daggers at him as we stepped into the fire's circle of light. "You went and made me too comfortable, you baneful man!" she chided.

"Your pains have started again."

"Yes. Hard. Too hard for anything to stop them now—Mr. Josh!" she called my father closer. A guttural groan escaped as she squeezed his arm. When she released him, I saw a welt appear. But he only smiled.

"Over?" he asked quietly.

"Yes, sir. Thank you."

Daddy Asher slipped his vial of lavender oil into my hand and took our harvest of leaves. "See what you can do, Lily," he said. "Your father and I must fetch water for the tea and poultice."

"Men!" Kikoyo groused as they disappeared into the shadows. "They don't mind so much being around when they get the babies started!"

We laughed together then. "Immoderate, Lily." I heard my sister's opinion of it in my head. "You're waking the children with that unladylike braying!" Jane? I sniffed the air for a better sense of her. I imagined her laughing at the shreds that were left of my lady's finery. I didn't mind. My heart soared at the thought of her laughter, even if I were the cause of it, like the girl stuck to the goose in the fairy tale— just so the princess, my sister, laughed. Ham's words brought me out of my reverie.

"Mama. You're bleeding."

A thin trickle of red flowed from Kikoy's lip. She wiped it quickly with her sleeve. "You and your brother must fetch and clean me a tasty root to chew on, instead of my lip, big sister," she said. The worry in her voice competed with the suffering, worry that she'd frighten her first two children in her effort to bring the third one forth.

"I need that trickster Irish man to tend my Ham and Delsey through my hard laboring, Miss Lily," she said, as I settled her back on her side in the pine needle bed. "Will that woman bring him soon?"

"Yes," I said, uncorking my grandfather's vial. "She likes to be around at birthing times."

Hugh came, with supplies and warm coverlets and a new look of peaceful serenity that I envied. The ferrywoman watched from her sloop as Kikoyo's labor progressed. I held cups of raspberry leaf tea to her lips, and rubbed lavender oil on her brow. I gave her my arm when she wanted to walk. Hugh even made us untie every tie in our clothing and possessions—to aid in the birth, he explained, an Irish birthing custom. We took the children to scour the island for natural ties in vines and such.

"Did your trip go well?" I asked him.

"Aye. Your Uncle Ross looks like Mr. Steenwyck."

"Yes. It's Charlie favors Gran Constance. Hugh, what did you first say to the ferrywoman when you came on board?"

I could see his mind reassembling his Irish language into one of my understanding, even as he scanned the raspberry bushes for anything that resembled a knot. "I said, 'Are you of the living or of the dead?' "

"My. And what was her answer?"

"She didn't answer, though I'd asked in the proper way. She said she placed her hope on the water, in her little boat."

I put my arm through his. Kikoyo cried out in pain. A knot! Hugh quickly unwound us. "Let's hold hands only, Lily," he urged, "leaving everything, even our arms, untied, open, to welcome the baby in."

Still Kikoyo could not seem to settle herself into bearing forth.

Finally, between hard and fast pains, she did burst some knots—her misgivings. "Miss Lily, forgive me, but you are barely more than a child. I want my own womenfolk. What if—? I got my Ham and Delsey. Them and Mr. North, they need me. I can't be dying here, in this lonely place full of spirits! I ain't pushing this baby out here!" she declared.

Hugh stepped into the firelight. He'd just been relieved of Ham and Delsey's care by my father and grandfather. In the distance, they were making music for the ferrywoman's delight.

"Why, do I hear you rightly, Mrs. North?" Hugh demanded. "Are you thinking my Lily can't catch your wee *bab*? Why, when she's fresh out of that women's-ways school of hers with all manner of learnin'?"

"About birth they taught you in that place, Miss Lily?" Kikoyo whispered, confused.

Before I could reply, Hugh continued with his badgering questions. "What else would a women's school teach, I'd like to know? Not the farming nor the fowling! Now, are you going to let her be about her work, or is her poor father going to be made poorer when the mistress of that place demands her return? And do you wish to go back to Mrs. Beech's school, Lily Woods?" he asked me.

"No!" I almost shouted. "I-I wish to go home to our mountains," I said more quietly, but still caught in the spell of Hugh Delaney's blarney.

Kikoyo, even in her exhausted state, was, too. She touched my hair. "I'm sorry, Miss Lily," she whispered. "I know you don't want to go back there." She stared off toward the moored sloop. "Don't my Delsey play her mouth organ something fine?" Just then a deluge of water burst from between her legs. "Ah. That's better. I believe we'd best get on with things now," she informed me, taking Hugh's arms and squatting over the coverlet we'd laid out.

After her first push, the baby's head crowned. With the second, a damp head emerged, with eyes that opened, blinking at me. I held out my hands. Shoulders eased themselves out. Seconds later the rest of Kikoyo's baby was in my arms, squirming and wailing softly. Kikoyo reached for my burden.

"What we got this time, Lily?" she asked softly.

"A son," I managed to whisper.

"Well." She laughed. "Come see your mama, child, she's got what you're looking for."

The baby blinked and turned toward Kikoyo's voice. The pulsing cord that still linked him to her stretched nicely as I relinquished him to his mother's arms and breasts. I'd been allowed to stand in the doorway watching almost a dozen births that the grandmothers attended. I knew the baby belonged in his mother's arms, suckling to help her bring forth the afterbirth. Still, it was hard to give this wondrous little body up.

I watched as Hugh reached down from his place behind Kikoyo. He offered his little finger, and the baby took a firm grasp.

"Jesus, Mary, Joseph, Padraig, Brigid, and all the saints forgive me for working such blarney on a birthing woman this night," he intoned softly.

The baby gurgled. My father, holding up Delsey and Ham in his arms behind me, laughed. "I expect they will, son," he assured him. "I expect even Kikoyo will."

As the children joined their mother and new brother, I felt my grandfather's hand on my shoulder. From between his two fingers dangled a steamed-soft strip of elm bark. "I believe we might start tying things again," he said, indicating the now flat, whitened cord that needed to be tied off. "With your Irishman's kind permission."

I was as weary as I'd ever felt in my life that night. Hugh was already asleep when my grandfather bundled me beside him. All the times Daddy Asher had raised coverlets over me—in the back rooms of Community House frolics, when my cousins and I spent the night with him and Gran, and out under the starry skies on mountain peaks—came dancing through my mind, filling me with an unspeakable joy. I watched the impatient flutter of the bit of cloth over his heart. It looked more red now, somehow. I reached out to touch it, but he caught my hand gently.

I was about to tease him for snatching a piece of Gran's hair ribbon when I realized there were tears in his eyes.

"You're so cold, Daddy Asher," I realized as I said it.

He tucked my hand under the coverlet. "Lily," he whispered. "I want you to remember something. I want you to tell it to your gran if ever she grows sad in your company."

"What, sir?"

"That this was the happiest day of my life."

"But why would Gran have cause—"

"Will you do that for me?"

"I will, sir."

"Thank you." He fixed me with that Catskill eagle stare of his. "I take a measureless pride in you, Lily Woods," he whispered, before he rose to his feet and walked silently out of the small fire's light.

He didn't mean for me to follow him, but the aching weariness in my limbs was now set aside for my need. Daddy must have had it, too, I reasoned as I heard him and his father speaking together on their walk to the mooring spot. I followed their footfalls, in that silent way I'd been taught. I was aided by the predawn mist swirling up my legs and shortened petticoats.

"Nathan will come by for you. He'll bring Mr. North, I think."

"Wait for them with us, Daddy. There's room by the fire."

"I cannot, Josh." Daddy Asher smiled gently. "This lady's been very patient already, hasn't she?"

"No!" The word exploded from my father's lips.

"Josh—" Daddy Asher tried calming him.

"She didn't come to claim you that night after the wolf bit you, Daddy. It . . . it took me a while, but I fashioned in my mind what really happened."

"Are you so sure of everything still, Justice Woods?"

"No! I'm not sure of anything. Daddy, stay."

"I think you must have had the makings of a fine lawyer, even then. And I'm grateful. But now it's time."

"She came to listen to the music is all, there at the house, when you turned gray, like the wolf," Daddy persisted. "For the music, not for you. She loves 'Honor to the Hills,' too!"

"Keep singing it, son."

Daddy's eyes shifted to those of the silent, watchful ferrywoman. Then, to my amazement, my father, who had braved so much over the last hours, began to weep. "No," he whispered. "Daddy, no."

"Hush, now," his father breathed. "The child, Josh." He pointed with his chin to where I stood stock-still among the raspberry vines. "Don't frighten your little girl."

My father nodded, wiping his eyes with the back of his hands. I waited until Daddy Asher stepped back from his son, the same quiet way he had from me, and boarded the small sloop. It disappeared in the mist. I approached the shore, took my father's hand, and pressed it to my face.

"He's in Sally Hamilton's care, Daddy," I tried to comfort him. "He'll be all right."

He granted me a whisper of a smile, though his eyes still ached in their misery. "I know, Lily. It's for the rest of us I worry."

25

HOME

Nathan sailed over to us that morning, just as Daddy Asher had said he would, bringing Mr. North to meet his island-born grandson. My uncle pronounced Kikoyo and her baby fit, but was concerned about his own brother. Daddy sat, glassy-eyed, as I held his hand and Uncle Nathan pulled out the stitches Captain Custis had put in his chin. Our gentle family doctor shook his head with dismay when he examined the purple bruises at Daddy's middle.

"We need to get you in bed, Josh," he pronounced.

"No. I need to see my mother, my family," he maintained, staring at our mountains.

My uncle pulled me aside. "Does he have any other injuries, Lily?" he asked me quietly. "Was he fevered in the night?"

"I don't think so, sir. But they had one of their arguments. I didn't understand this one at all."

"Argument?"

"Yes. Daddy Asher said—"

"Daddy? He was here?"

"Sure. Didn't he tell you he was coming to the dock? To meet the *Artemis?* When he heard of the wreck—"

"Lily. My father's in the mountains." He looked over his shoulder, as if forgetting that we were in a place where no authorities could overhear what he said next. He took my arm in his light hold. "Josh talked to you? About the family . . . venture on the northern rail line?"

"Yes, but what does that have to do—"

"Daddy is delivering a shipment though the gap you two worked over Second Sister. I wanted to go, too. The bounty hunters who'd missed the race to get Kikoyo are still sniffing about, you see. So are the Chases. But Mama sent me to meet the boat. She said she dreamed about burning water."

"The wreck."

"Yes. You know your gran and her dreams."

"But Daddy Asher wasn't a dream. He was here, Uncle Nathan."

"I don't see how that's possible."

"He was here, he and Sally Hamilton both."

My uncle went pale. "Sally Hamilton?" he whispered. "She came for him again?"

"She came for all of us—before the boat went down."

"Lily," he breathed, taking my face in his hand, as if to be sure I was solid and not a thing of air. It frightened me, but I hid my fear in nervous laughter.

"Look," I called, remembering physical evidence I had of Daddy Asher's rescue. "His vial of lavender oil. From his medicine bag, Uncle Nathan." I shoved my hand into the deep pocket inside the shreds of my silk dress and pulled out my grandfather's lavender-oil vial.

My uncle smiled at the sight of it. "That certainly looks like one of his." he affirmed. "But Lily, he'd have to have flown off the mountains to have—"

"Don't say that to Daddy, Uncle Nathan. He's so worried as it is!" I pleaded, both for my father's sake and my own.

"Of course," he said, still uneasy. "We'll clear this all up when we get home, won't we?"

"Yes. Home."

The word did not have its usual steadying effect on me.

In Catskill, Mr. North and Annie made ready to board in town with Kikoyo for a short confinement before they'd bring her and her children over the mountain to home.

Before we parted, Kikoyo put her baby in my arms. "We figure to see how the name your granddaddy gave him sticks to this child, Miss Lily," she said, in as shy a voice as I'd ever heard from her.

"Name?" I said, perplexed.

"Freeman, he said, remember? So this is Freeman North."

I looked down into the lovely sleeping face, but all I could think of was that my grandfather had never held him. Why not? He loved babies. And why had his hands been so cold of a summer's night?

"Does it please you, the name?" Kikoyo asked, perplexed.

"Lily?" Hugh called me then, his face concerned. I placed the baby in his arms. He held him easily, the way Daddy Asher held babies. I clung to my father's arm, feeling as confused and frail as that girl who was my disguised self on the New York City dock.

Kikoyo looked from me to my father. "You won't have cause to regret us in your household, Justice Woods," she said. "And my babies, they don't holler much at all. Will you tell your lady that, sir?"

"Freeman won't have a chance to so much as sniffle," he maintained, almost sounding like himself again. "There will be so many arms to hold him." He backed away from the family that had added a member that day. "We'll see you all in a little while. Lily? Hugh?"

Hugh released his burden. We hugged Delsey and Ham good-bye.

The town of Stony Clove looked different when we arrived. We all felt it. Folks going about their daily business looked up, but did not meet our eyes. A long cloak Uncle Nathan had procured for me in Catskill covered all my torn and frayed finery. I wasn't the cause of the stares. We were shunned equally, as if we'd brought home a catching sickness.

"Something's happened," Uncle Nathan said as we approached his town house. "Wait here," he instructed us all, but in a tone that also commanded Hugh and me to look after my father, sitting too straight in the saddle, his eyes pained. Minutes later, Uncle Nathan flew out his front door, a note in Aunt Pen's handwriting grasped in his fist. He remounted, his face set, grim. "Everyone's at the big house," he said. "That's all she writes."

Daddy nodded, and turned his horse toward home.

Carriages, carts, or horses accounting for every member of my family were indeed at the big house. All of Daddy Asher's soldier families were there, too, as well as two rigs from Mr. North's folks. It looked like a wedding or birthday. But it was still a week from the big celebration we have every year to honor Daddy and Aunt Susannah's joint coming into the world under a sky full of bright stars.

Aunt Susannah was sitting on the front portico steps, a slim armband of grief discordant against her blue sleeve. She ran to take Daddy and Nathan into her embrace.

"Gone from us," her tear-choked voice told them, "doing what he liked to do best in the world."

As I dismounted I heard my mother call my name. Hugh's arms found another trial for their strength as my knees refused to hold my weight.

"I've got you, Lily," he whispered against my hair.

Aunt Susannah gave up her hold on her twin as Mama gathered Daddy, Hugh, and me into her embrace. "Thank God," I heard her whisper. She held us as if we'd disappear. "I thought I'd lost you all."

"Let them come inside, Mother. Let's put them all to bed."

I raised my eyes to Jane, standing tall and beautiful beside Cousin Gerald. She was my sister again, stroking my face with her bandaged fingers as I closed my eyes against the steady heartbeat in Hugh Delaney's chest.

Everyone said my grandfather's sitting was the best in the valley since Quinn Delaney's, back in the year without a summer, when my father was my age. I like to think that was because we had another Delaney in the house, prompting Daddy Asher stories from everyone who dropped by to leave a dish of supper or five-stack apple cake.

The story of my grandfather's death was a simple one. It took place on Second Sister and was caused by a rifle shot, through his heart, while he was lifting a child over a ridge. When he examined his father's body, Uncle Nathan said there was only a trickle of blood staining his billowy shirt, the shot had been so clean, the death so quickly achieved. Daddy Asher had barely time to place the child safely in her mother's arms before he fell, the folks who were with him said. Signs showed that when they realized they'd killed a white man, the riflemen left off their pursuit in fear of retaliation. Asher Woods, who'd been called a heathen savage all his life, taken for a white man. That had allowed the runaways to achieve their next station. Maybe he'd find that amusing.

The flight of his killers allowed two members of the runaway team time to bring Daddy Asher's body home to Gran. It was brave of them, but they said they could do no less. They said they would tell the story of his passing over and over so that it would be a difficult thing for even the hardest-used of slaves to hate all Americans because of what this one had done for their sake.

I listened to their story just before they headed north to join their party in Plattsburg, packed with bundles of food that were arriving with folks for the sitting.

I missed a good deal of the sitting, or wake, as Hugh called it, being sent to bed by a mother and sister who were taking no chances with the gifts to have come out of the family's dark night. That's what Mama took to calling Daddy and Hugh and me in our return to her. Everyone, especially Gran, doted on us, and worked with a will toward our care. I, who could not recall ever being in a sickbed before, got to see the other side of need—the need of our grief-stricken caretakers to feel useful.

Mama commanded that all the doors of our house be left open for the whole week, so Daddy and I could hear Mr. Tinkor's bright fiddle playing and all the laughter from our recovery beds. And we had Hugh and his full, robust reports of all the stories from our steady stream of visitors. When I think of that time, it is in Hugh's manner of telling, his speech, his cadence.

Hugh Delaney began the long road to his own literacy there beside my sickbed, a slate in his big workman's hands turning, over time, to paper and pen, the grammar book, and reading for himself the battles fought over Helen, the woman he still calls "that Grecian queen." His manner of speech breaks "Grecian" into three well-rung Irish syllables.

It was a year before I first had cause to tell Gran what Daddy Asher had charged me.

Jane had married Cousin Gerald, a wedding we all rejoiced in, even Daddy, though this second Griffin link made the Widow Webber and cousin Wilhemina permanent month-long summer visitors to our home, their "rustic mountain retreat." In that summer of 1852, Jane was six months heavy with my parents' first grandchild.

Failed compromises continued in Washington. Daddy worked in the courts for personal-liberty laws that will sometimes prohibit state and local officers from obeying the national fugitive slave law. The Underground Railroad was still very much with us.

Jane's being with child had not quenched her fire for saving the world from itself. She'd enlisted my help on her new project, one that suited my nature better: taking down the narratives of freedmen and women who told me stories of their lives in slavery. I loved the work, though of course my sister and I had our differences about the manner of its presentation—Jane insisting I must make the language of the stories sound like they were book-learned white people so as not to add fuel to the fire of those with claims of natural inferiority.

"Let any who think that way come and visit Mr. North's forge," I protested, "or see Ham and Delsey at their lessons, or see how Kikoyo runs our household, Jane. But don't have me change the rich music of their talk!"

She tapped her fingers against the apron tie at her high waist, the way she'd taken to doing when she was running out of patience with me.

"It's not talk, it's literature once in print, Lily."

Hugh heard our argument as he sat eating Kikoyo's raspberry tarts. Once my sister had left, he provided a solution—that I make two copies of each interview, one for Jane and the abolitionist pamphlets and newspapers, and another to place "in the priest hole," as he still calls the secret place beside our hearth.

Hugh and I had trudged up to Gran's cabin for another bottle of her chestnut ink with Delsey and Ham and a toddling Freeman when we discovered her crying at the table in her kitchen. I sent Hugh with the children on to pick blueberries while I sat with my grandmother.

"He lived longer than any member of his family ever got to," she told me through her tears as I poured her tea. "He marveled at that so many times after the wolf bites almost killed him that night."

I sat beside her. "And he died on the happiest day of his life, Gran. He charged me to tell you that whenever you take to grieving."

She stared at me, her eyes wide as a child's. "Did he, Lily? On that night on Turtle Island?"

"Yes, ma'am." I watched her sip a little of the tea before I ventured to ask the question I'd been wondering about for many months. "Where's your red hair ribbon, Gran?"

She put down the cup and looked out the window, smiling at the sound of the children's laughter. She considered more before she spoke again. "Lily, the feelings you have for Hugh—they are very strong, aren't they?"

"Oh, yes."

"With the right man, they do not change over the years, but grow, deepen. They are the feelings Asher Woods and I had for each other all our lives—that rush of blood when he walked in the room, swung a child or a grandchild or even a rifle to his shoulder. The smell of him at sugaring time, rich and warm and sweet as the maple's flow. When he pulled the ribbon from my hair that morning and our bodies joined, it was like the first time, deep in the night on the shores of Echo Lake, where he'd brought me to escape the torments of the wedding pranksters. Imagine that, darling Lily? Like the first time, only deeper, richer, for us old and seasoned lovers. I never opened the box that holds my ribbon again."

"Let's open it now, Gran," I urged.

When she did, her face became one she'd leveled on Daddy Asher many times when he'd angered her. She held up the sliced-in-half bit of shining red to the light and fisted her other hand at her waist. "That man!" she growled. "Does he think me so poor-sighted I'd not be able to find him again without a token?"

Hugh said it was the look on my face after that visit with Gran that made him bend a knee and ask for my hand before he'd planned on it. His sprightly good nature had joined with his growing ability to read and won him a foreman's job at the free-labor cotton mill. With it came a family man's wages. But he insisted he'd not made himself nearly interesting enough to gain my returned affections. It was a foolish notion, of course, for he'd had my affections since I'd pitched him off that place we were standing. No, not pitched. I never pitched him off any precipice! Hark at this, he's got me writing his blarney as my own, that baneful man!

The clouds over Second Sister rolled overhead and suddenly spilled out a deluge, making my poor suitor wait for his answer until we'd achieved the cover of the big house's front portico.

"You'd better marry me, Hugh Delaney," I charged him then, wet and breathless from our run. "You're the only bachelor who's seen me dressed down to a single petticoat."

He frowned, looking worried. "That's not the truth of it. Your daddy's sailor Mr. Bingham has, too. And he's come to visit twice since his recovery."

I laughed. "I don't want a husband who plows the seas, Hugh. I want one who can charm my babies."

His fine hand took hold of my face so tenderly then. "Could we name one for my sister, Lily?" he asked.

"Our first girl," I promised.

He leaned closer, his face illuminated by a flash of summer lightning. I raised myself on my toes to receive his kiss, but felt only the whisper of his lips on mine before my father opened the door.

Looking a little desperate, he pulled Hugh and me inside. "Ah, this is fine, just the two voices we need to fill out the chorus!" he exclaimed.

Hugh tried to slip out of Daddy's grip. "Terrible storm, sir. I ought to go calm down the horses." He wanted to get out of an audience with my downriver relatives. The horses were always Daddy Asher's last defense when in similar circumstances. Hugh saw defeat nearing in the person of my mother, pleased as always to greet him.

"Mr. Steenwyck was just asking about our Hugh," Mama said, ignoring the grass stains on his shirt and knees where he'd roughhoused with the children. "He and Gran Constance are here"—she began listing allies to counter our more unpleasant guests—"along with Nathan's family, and most of Susannah's. You'll give us the pleasure of a few verses of 'Honor to the Hills' and a small supper afterward, Hugh?" she asked in that plaintive Scottish lilt that my father says melts away the rocks at planting time.

Hugh took up her extended hand. "If Lily leads," he half acceded, half challenged.

Mama winced when a voice crackling with displeasure sounded behind her.

"My, what travails has our young Lily suffered to arrive home in such a soaked, bedraggled state?" Aunt Webber exclaimed in horror. Cousin Wilhemina giggled at her side.

Uncle Nathan and Aunt Pen came to our rescue. Aunt Pen's arm slipped through Hugh's, while my uncle's hand rested on my shoulder.

"They have no doubt been gathering medicinals for me, dear ladies."

"Indeed?"

"Hugh adds to our knowledge with Irish uses for our roots and plants. And Lily accompanies me on visits to my patients as well. She has been so compassionate an assistant that I'm thinking of sponsoring her in a course of study at Columbia, Mrs. Webber," he said with a sly grin.

"A woman physician, sir? Surely I have lived too long if such a thing is possible!"

"It is a reality, madame, though, sadly, still a rare one."

The old woman frowned. "Jane's insistence on founding a new academy was troublesome enough, though I'm glad to see it's in a more proper place here on this wilderness side of the river, where radical ideas are better tolerated. But Lily a physician? I am still getting used to the notion of women teaching. What do you think of it, young man?" she called on Hugh, who was eyeing the corn pudding.

Hugh gave the ancient widow of the Revolution a little bow. "Why wouldn't I cast my lot with Nathan Woods, who brought me back from the door of death itself, Mrs. Webber?" he asked. "I'd be an ungrateful wretch if ever I'd do so! And if the family's book-learned doctor says he's got his best skills from the grandmothers, seems Lily comes by it naturally. Do you follow the line to the place my thoughts are taking me, good lady, or is my expression too poor for such a grand personage as yourself?" He flashed her a grin that reminded me of Daddy Asher's.

"You have made yourself understood, Mr. Delaney," she admitted with a small ruffle of her voluminous black skirts.

"And doesn't that gladden my heart like the blue air in these high hills?"

She took his hand and pulled him to her. "Do you find the mountains restorative, too, sir?" she asked, as if Hugh was suddenly transformed into a grand personage himself. I stifled my spurt of laughter behind my hand while my town-, city-, and estate-bred relatives all looked on in awe.

I was selfishly glad the company's attention went to Hugh, long enough for me to race up the back stairs and change my muddied clothing. From my room I heard laughter and knew Hugh was charming my Griffin relatives, despite his aversion to people even Mama says are a trial in their formal pomposity. When I slipped down the back stairs to the kitchen, Delsey and Ham were peeking out the swinging door to the dining room as their mother entered with a tray.

"In good time, Lily!" Kikoyo called. "They're setting up chairs now, and Mr. Steenwyck's pitch pipe's at the ready. Turn around quick and let me straighten your chignon." She opened the door no wider than a crack and gave her next report. "Your auntie's got her handkerchief out in surrender, so they'll be singing soon."

"I'll get my mouth organ, Lily!" Delsey volunteered.

"Not tonight, child," her mother said.

"You're all welcome, Kikoyo," I urged, but she shook her head.

"I expect this horde is shocking the Griffins enough without us mixing in." She smiled slyly. "Tonight, anyway," she reconsidered before turning her attention to the children again. "It's time for you two to join Freeman and Dr. Nathan's little ones under the covers in there. Go on, now. We'll let these Woods people and their soaring voices sing you to sleep." I received my good-night hugs before Kikoyo put a tray in my hands. "I need to hear their prayers, so they remember their ancestors as well as your Jesus and Moses and all. Lily, set out the tarts," she commanded, looking over my shoulder. "And see that your young man stays out of the clutches of that fussy cousin of yours!" She headed for the children's room with them in tow.

As I set down the tarts beside the corn pudding, I thought of Uncle Nathan praising me. Did he merely mean to pique the widow? No, that was not his nature. Could the healing powers that had passed from female hands into his own be going toward mine next? I could think of nothing more wonderful than roaming these mountains with him in that service. And Hugh, for all his blarney, seemed proud of the notion of being a husband to a healer woman.

' I thought of these things while we tuned our voices and sat in our hollow four-square formation. "Lily?" Hugh reminded me of my leader's place, standing in the middle with a graceful turn of his arm. I took it, and looked with measureless pride at the members of my family surrounding me, waiting for my signal to begin.

Daddy, Hugh, and Gerald took the tenor section. Learning the shape-note singing our family loved was one of the ways Gerald and Hugh paid Jane and me court, but I think both would have taken to the songs all on their own. Uncle Nathan, Susannah's husband Gilbert Jenkins, and Mr. Steenwyck took up the bass, while Mama and Aunt

Pen and cousin Charlotte had a good grasp on the alto. Gran Constance and Aunt Susannah were lonely trebles without Gran. I felt an immensity of sadness burden my heart then, as I realized we'd carefully avoided singing Daddy Asher's favorite hymn since we'd lost him. Only Hugh's fair face nodding helped me find my courage.

" 'Honor to the Hills,' verses one, three and four," I said, raising my hand to signal our beginning. Once the words rose high, nothing but the sound and sense of the music mattered.

> *"Through all this world below, God we see all around*
> *Search hills and valleys through, there He's found*
> *In growing fields of corn, the lily and the thorn,*
> *The pleasant and forlorn,*
> *All declare God is there*
> *In meadows dress'd in green, there He's seen."*

As our voices rang out, I imagined them bringing a family welcome to Hugh Delaney, telling him not to be afraid among us hill dwellers, that he might even find God among us.

> *"The sun with all his rays, speaks of God as he flies:*
> *The comet in its blaze, God it cries.*
> *The shining of the stars, the moon when she appears,*
> *His dreadful name declares:*
> *See them fly through the sky,*
> *And join the silent sound from the ground."*

"What manner of music is this?" the Widow Webber cried out, interrupting us. It took us all the brief silence to realize that the widow's and her niece's reaction was one of dismayed shock. "That . . . is not the sort of hymn we sing in our congregation," she gasped.

"Nor here, dear lady!" Mr. Steenwyck assured her. "Oh, we sang the shape-note songs in church back in the first settlement days, but they're now unsuitable for today's predictable harmonies."

"I daresay! A style so independent, dissonant . . . well, so emotional, would detract from the proper spirit of worship!"

"But isn't the proper spirit of worship served by passion?" my father asked in his best lawyer's tone of inquiry.

I smiled, taking up his case. "The letters we receive from Reuben and Tascha are full of reports that the shape-note singing tradition flourishes in the western wilderness among settlers there."

"I daresay," the Widow Webber said with a soft snort.

"We still sing the shape-note songs at home, and in crossroads," Mr. Steenwyck maintained, rising like a lean, grand patriarch from his place, "even though they are deemed too earthy, untamed." He grinned. "Rather like our Asher." He looked around, suddenly confused. "Where's Asher?" he asked us just as Gran slipped into the room. "Ginny," he called, before any could stop him, "where's our Asher?"

Gran smiled. "Listening, Mr. Steenwyck," she told her stepfather gently as she sat beside Aunt Susannah. "Shall we finish, Lily?"

I closed my eyes to better let the diverse voices of the people I loved best in the world blend into my being as we sang together.

> "Then let my station be, here in life, where I see
> The sacred Trinity all agree,
> In all the works He's made, the forest and the glade,
> Nor let me be afraid,
> Though I dwell on the hill,
> Where nature's works declare God is there."

J
FIC
CHAR

change to YA

2954 6

Charbonneau, Eileen

Honor to the Hills

DELETE/WITHDRAWN
EAST CHELTENHAM FREE LIBRARY
400 MYRTLE AVENUE
CHELTENHAM, PA 19012-2038

1695

GAYLORD FG